BROKEN

A. L. FRANCES

Ruby Rose Publishing

Ruby Rose Publishing House PAPERBACK

© Copyright 2020
A. L. Frances

A CIP catalogue record for this title is
available from the British Library.

ISBN 978-0-9601051-0-6

The Broken is an imprint of
Ruby Rose Publishing House.
www.RubyRosePublishingHouse.com

First Published in 2020

Printed & Bound in Great Britain and United States of America

AUTHOR NOTE

My purpose for writing the series of *The Broken* novels extends above and beyond just wanting to write a gripping, close-to-home story.

On occasions, I've picked up books and been unable to visualise what the writer has so beautifully written for me. Then, when I've found a book I've loved and read it to the end, the sense of achievement is immeasurable. I believe everyone should embrace this emotion when they read.

My desire is for you to feel just as wonderful when you reach the end of this novel, as I've written this wholeheartedly for you!

DEDICATION

I wrote this for you…

A. L. Frances

CONTENTS

The world that we are blessed to embrace every living day seems so pure when we follow the positive teachings nature has to offer.

This colourful planet that beautifully homes our life as we know it, is populated by approximately 7.5 billion people. I'm sure you'll agree with me, that's one large number!

Every day, people meet new people; our human race is very trusting. We invite people into our lives, we invite people into our families, our homes, our businesses, without truly knowing them.

When we add new people to our lives, what I believe we should be asking ourselves is: what's this person's intention?

Are their intentions the same as mine, or do they appear to have a motive for being present in my life at this very moment?

We are all at risk of being used by people; if we, as adults, invite them into our lives, then so be it for us, agreed? Now the plot begins to thicken somewhat, if we, as adults, have a family living with us and we invite this new person into our family dimension. Would you then agree that this changes things slightly?

Well, what about the family set-ups where one parent isn't present?

Single parents can be especially vulnerable to people who may not have the best intentions. Single parents sometimes look to fill the void of the missing family link – the other parent.

If it's within your desires, being a parent is a wonderful gift that the majority of the population are blessed to embrace. Sharing this special gift with another, be that a biological parent or someone you feel that you've carefully selected, should be a process you give gratitude for as your family unit grows. I'm sure you would agree to that one, too.

Can you imagine? You've invited another person into your life with faith, belief and the trust that their soul is the right match for yours. You share your life, you share your home, you share your journey, and you share the souls of your dependants with this person. Not only do you trust them to bring positive influences and kindness into your home, you may also expect them to fill the gap of the missing role model for your dependants.

Could you imagine going to all that effort only to fall victim to this person you have so carefully chosen? But hang on a minute, it's not just you who will fall victim – the dependants that you have in your life fall victim, too, all because *you*, the adult, said yes to this person being a part of all your lives.

.

CHAPTER ONE

The Honeys

The day is bright, breezy and full of hope. Matthew Honey is standing in the living room of his luxury three-storey home, which overlooks the beautiful serenity of a small, blissful English beach and is positioned perfectly just outside the centre of Hythe, south of London in Folkestone, Kent. The room he stands in is grand, light and airy. Every object has its own place; not a single item leans so much as a centimetre out of place. This beautiful building with its strong structure stands out from the crowded beach front. A vision of architectural beauty, this house truly has the wow factor. Two solid stone white pillars that are at least twenty feet high give the entrance a grand and extravagant impression. The deep brown mahogany front door has been crafted to perfection, with gold trimmings. The arched entrance to the house really sets it apart from the others on the sea front. An enormous window is positioned above the doorway. The house's unique, luxurious exterior was designed by Matthew and Lauren Honey. They had an image in their minds of the home they desired to raise their young in; from that vision, this magnificent building with its fresh brown brick and multiple huge windows was constructed.

At forty-seven, Matthew Honey is a young widow. He wears an expensive blue tailored suit, designed to fit his slim and toned body to perfection. His dark hair, which has a slight curl to it, is slicked back, with strands of grey peering through on either side.

Standing with his back to the tall, immaculate, white living room door, he gazes peacefully out of the window at the sea. He looks up to the piercing blue, crystal-clear sky and watches as delicate white clouds drift gracefully by, a subtle reminder that the world is continually passing with ease. A gentle smile begins to form on Matthew's handsome face as he sees two seagulls glide overhead. Reaching up to the collar of his white, crisp shirt, he corrects his tie. Once he has perfected his appearance, Matthew takes a deep breath, almost filling his lungs; then pushes the air from his body in a huge sigh: a sigh of relief, a sigh of despair, a sigh of forgiveness, who knows?

Closing his eyes to embrace the moment, Matthew senses vibrations from the floor beneath him. As he is partially deaf in his right ear, he has increased sensitivity to vibrations in the environment around him. His body now absorbs the tingling sensation, his nerves reacting to the movement. Matthew can now hear the stampede-like footsteps coming from behind him. He seems unalarmed by the noise. A voice calls out, clear as day, "There you are!"

Immediately, Matthew begins to smile; he knows exactly who these elephant feet belong to.

Turning slightly to look over his shoulder, he sees his miracle, his blessing, his beautiful one and only daughter, Eve. She's dressed extremely smartly for a sixteen-year-old girl in a deep grey fitted suit with a white blouse. Her make-up has been painstakingly applied to her face. It must have taken hours. With her hair pulled back into a bun on the top of her head and a black pair of kitten heels on her feet, she has mastered the corporate look.

Matthew beams with pride as he looks directly at his lifesaver, who stands in the doorway looking somewhat concerned and slightly frustrated at her dad's lack of response. Waving her arms around in an *is-anybody-home* gesture she says, "Erm, hello, Dad… We're going to be late at this rate."

He walks across the room to Eve and places his hand under her chin. You could spend an eternity searching the entire universe and you would struggle to find a bond tighter than exists between this father and his daughter. His eyes oozing love and his heart beginning to warm, he replies, "Eve, you worry far too much."

Eve tuts and raises her eyebrows. "Well, someone has to," she responds, rolling her eyes.

Smiling at her mocking yet heartfelt words, Matthew glances down at the glistening necklace visible through the gap in her blouse. Closing his eyes, he feels an immediate sense of discomfort and agony as he hears a pained scream in his mind; not just any scream, it's the high-pitched screaming of a suffering child, hurting internally and externally. Quickly opening his eyes, Matthew looks at his daughter and holds her tight. Eve doesn't question this, giving in to the embrace.

Releasing Eve from his arms, Matthew cups the heart-shaped locket hanging on the white-gold necklace, a vision of beauty in its simplistic elegance and filled with deep memories of the irreplaceable kind. As tears of sorrow form in his eyes, he relives a precious memory.

Eve is standing on her tippy toes, balancing on a white-painted wooden chair next to the solid mahogany island in the centre of the kitchen. The chair she is standing on so innocently in her excitement is special and has been hand-crafted especially for her. On the seat is a detailed painting of a magical purple and pink unicorn. On the back, Evelyn Jade is carved into the wood, painted with luminous pink paint and sprinkled with what Eve would call her magical fairy dust, which is actually silver glitter. This is a very blessed child, who has two very loving parents.

She's wearing a mucky pinafore and her facial expression is pure and sweet. Matching plaits are draped over her shoulders, hanging either side of her tiny infant features. Eve's usual cheeky grin is plastered across her face. She's clapping her tiny hands together and dry white flour fills the air, spreading around the kitchen. It coats everything it lands on, like snow on a winter's night.

Lauren reaches out to their precious daughter and playfully presses cake mix on the tip of her nose. She looks her usual radiant, happy,

3

beautiful self. A twinkle comes from the necklace hanging around his wife's neck...

... the very same necklace that Eve now proudly wears. He closes his eyes tight, embracing the memory, but removes himself from the moment. It's too painful to relive.

Eve looks up at her dad and says these simple yet heart-wrenching words: "I miss her."

"Evelyn Jade Honey, you remind me of her every day. Your mum would be so proud of the beautiful, courageous, strong young lady you've become, I know it."

Matthew acknowledges that he's been lost since he was forced to say goodbye to his wife, his soul mate. From that day on, he became nothing more than a wandering lost soul, destined not to live but merely to exist. Without this amazing woman, he feels he is nothing. Snapping out of the moment before he cries uncontrollably, Matthew holds Eve and says, "Let's go to the café."

Having regained his composure, he stares proudly at his daughter.

She frowns and says, "But... your meeting?"

Matthew smiles ever so gently. He's gone from the depths of despair, wondering why he's alive, to staring at his blessing, the reason he lives.

"Eve, you should know me by now. Two words: *extra hour...*"

Squinting her eyes, she reaches out and gently taps him on the arm in a cheeky manner. Every time Matthew has a meeting, or an event, he tells Eve the time is an hour earlier than it actually is, or he has to deal with her chasing him. Matthew's view is that taking your time is a much more productive and effective way to function. Since going through the traumatic experience of losing his wife, he doesn't like rushing, or being rushed. It's now a huge pet hate of his. Life is too short, and Matthew has absolutely no desire to spend any of his time stressed out, anxious or upset. Shaking her head, Eve hugs her dad and says, "Café it is, then."

As he drives along the country roads in his brand new, immaculate, shark-grey Porsche Cayenne, kitted out with full cream leather interior, Matthew looks over at Eve. She has her elbow resting gently on the window, her chin relaxing on her hand as she gazes up at the canopy of trees. They stand strong, forming an arch on each side that meet in the middle. A true vision of beauty. The sun's natural glow peeps through the tiny gaps between the leaves, creating a magical effect.

The journey is serene, the roads are clear. For Matthew life is in the air, along with a bright feeling, the feeling that anything can happen, endless possibilities, wonderful new beginnings. They've been through the worst thing any living person could imagine going through – losing a loved one; surely, life could only get better.

Matthew thinks back to a time when the words *losing a loved one* used to make him think of losing an elderly relative or a friend to a tragic illness. But the soul that he and Eve so tragically lost wasn't just anyone. Their loved one was once present in their lives every day. She was very cruelly and abruptly taken away. No time to say goodbye, no notification, nothing! She was taken by circumstances out of their control; completely powerless, they had to stand by and watch. As he drives through the peaceful countryside, Matthew reflects on the bitter sadness of having to continue his life without her magic and beauty every single day. Really, what could be worse than that?

Matthew looks again at Eve, who continues to stare out the window. He recalls that there were times when their relationship was very strained. They never understood each other well, they never made time to get to know each other. As the years went by and Eve grew up, Matthew thought she was a complete pain in the butt, especially when she hit puberty. And Eve probably thought he was old, uninteresting and a complete embarrassment, he thinks to himself, shaking his head wryly.

But going through a mentally traumatic experience and only having each other to lean on, mourn with and keep going for had brought them closer than he could have ever imagined. He was physically and mentally dragged away from his wife, and Eve was separated in the same manner from her mum. This tragedy gave them a strong connection once they finally pulled together. When he had no desire to live this constantly horrific and pained existence, Eve was the energy that lifted his soul, and vice versa.

Eve flicks on the radio. A familiar song begins to play throughout the car. It's the greatest hits of the eighties hour. Matthew looks over at her. The music makes her smile and she begins to dance theatrically, singing along to the music. Admittedly, her dance moves aren't the best and actually, to be honest, they're kind of tragic. But this has never stopped her before and it's certainly not going to stop her now as she continues without a care in the world. She is strapped tightly in her seatbelt and dancing on the spot. Her eyes are closed and she's singing the lyrics, moving around like no-one's watching. Opening her eyes, Eve says, "I love this song."

"How do you know this song? This is mine and your mum's era."

Laughing cheekily, she continues to sing. "Don't worry Dad, I haven't been going through your lame music collection, "she says.

"Oi, leave it out, you cheeky bugger. My music collection is classic."

She makes an expression of mock shock at her dad's name calling. "We've been learning about this in music class. How cruel is this, right – did you know it's actually about a blind woman? I mean, hello, she's blind, for God's sake. Not being funny, Dad, but I think the guy who wrote this is a little bit sick."

Matthew laughs at her innocence.

"Our music group has been chosen to perform this song at the end of year concert."

Pulling up at the traffic lights, Matthew quickly turns his attention to Eve.

As clear as day, he can remember sitting at the breakfast bar, deep in thought checking his accounts. And Eve, peering around the fridge door with a packet of wafer-thin ham in her hand, munching away as she says, "Don't forget, it's my end of year concert on the seventh of July. It's starting at two thirty and this year it's a… wait for it… Sunday. Yay. So, you should definitely be able to come."

He sits stiff in the driver's seat, both hands clutching the steering wheel. His face oozes guilt.

"You are coming, aren't you?"

Matthew attempts to appear somewhat confident, but a look of worry begins to spread across his face. He rarely gets to attend Eve's performances due to his demanding work commitments. Ordinarily, she's very forgiving, but this is her last ever end of year concert as she leaves school this year.

"Dad, you must be there, it's my last performance – you've missed every single one."

"Yes, of course, darling – I wouldn't miss it for the world."

Eve nods, seemingly satisfied with his words. The traffic lights turn green and they both start nodding and singing in sync with the music blasting through the car as they drive away.

CHAPTER TWO

The Meeting

Arriving at the café, they pull up in the car park at the side of the building. A huge sign stands at the entrance: *Private Car Park – Customers of Sunnyside Up Café Only*. The street is packed. People are everywhere; they're all rushing past each other with bags in their hands, and no one is smiling. Children run beside their parents, desperately trying to keep up. Matthew hops out of the car and takes a deep breath in, embracing the vision of the Honey family's most treasured place to eat out.

He walks around the car and sees Eve smiling. She appears to be day-dreaming.

"Come on then, kidda," he says.

She walks over to her dad with a big genuine grin spread across her face. Linked arm in arm, they form a vision of strength as they make their way towards the café.

The smell of cooking bacon, sausages and fresh coffee awakens their nostrils as they walk through the door. There are two young girls behind the counter, looking flustered in their grease-stained pinafores, their hair tied up tight. It's clear that these two would rather be anywhere but behind the counter right now, as the café is starting to get busy. As they rush around working on a customer's order, the girls notice Matthew and Eve and acknowledge them with sincere smiles.

"Hi, Matthew. Hi, Eve," says one.

"Eve! My God, I haven't seen you for ages – I'll come over and see you shortly," says the other.

"Okay. Hey, Sophie," Eve replies.

"Hi, Lucy. Hi, Sophie. Is your mum or dad about?" Matthew asks.

"No – they're still on a cruise, ain't they?" Sophie responds.

"Oh yeah – I forgot. Are they enjoying their exciting travelling experience?"

"They're lovin' it – last I heard they don't wanna come back. I told 'em they better, I want me life back. Suppose it's all right for some, aye."

"Ha, well, when you speak to them next, please let them know I was asking after them."

"Sure – will do."

The café is family run; it's really nothing spectacular and could probably do with a lick of paint. Being a very wealthy man, Matthew could take Eve to any café or fancy restaurant in any location on the globe. They can afford all the lavish luxuries they desire. But they stand by this family run café and will visit until the day they are taken from this beautiful planet. All those other cafés, restaurants and luxurious locations don't hold the one irreplaceable thing that this café holds: memories. They weren't always wealthy; Matthew and Lauren built their empire together, and before their days of wealth, this café was where they would come to mastermind. To them the café was "The Creative Station". They were never mithered, always welcomed, treated like family, and so they kept up the connection with the place. They would often have business meetings here, even long after their success. It was their lucky charm, a place of zen.

Eve takes a seat in their usual spot, "The Mastermind Corner". As she sits, Matthew makes his way over to the counter. Lucy and Sophie are already preparing his order before he arrives; now that's what you call a regular customer – loyal to the service and the service loyal to him. Sophie and Lucy's parents own the café and they've grown up with Matthew around. He has always been a regular, even before he got married and was a single young man without a care in the world. Matthew would come in the café with treats and give them to Lucy and Sophie, but not before he pretended he'd found them behind their ears. They saw him develop into a husband with a loving family, and they played with Eve as she was growing up. They've seen him a broken man at the depths of despair, trying desperately to live a *normal* life as a single dad, whilst working to keep the empire and legacy he built with his wife alive. Matthew is exchanging pleasantries with Lucy and Sophie when suddenly he feels a strong presence behind him.

The hairs stand up on the back of his neck and he freezes. He turns around and is stunned by the person standing there staring back. Standing proudly, with her head held high and shoulders back, is the most elegant woman he has ever seen. Her smile is radiant and welcoming and her energy beams brighter than a cluster of stars.

Matthew is lost for words. His mouth has dried up with nerves. He takes in her flowing dark brown hair, her slight freckles and perfectly painted nude plump lips. She has a natural, enchanting beauty. Just as the situation is getting slightly awkward, she says, "Are you okay?"

Unable to reply, Matthew continues to gaze in admiration at this woman. She's wearing a low-cut cream blouse, dark skinny jeans and fabulous nude stilettos. Hanging over one arm is an oversized beige handbag, a pile of paperwork clutched close to her body in the other.

Matthew's eyes are drawn by a glimmer to her slim neck, where there hangs a white-gold necklace. Suspended from this delicate chain is a striking silver heart-shaped locket. It is similar, if not identical, to the one Eve now has.

Tucking her hair behind her ear, she asks with her sophisticated voice, "Excuse me, are you okay...?"

"You are beautiful," Matthew finally says, although he probably wishes his brain had processed the words first. He instantly turns red with embarrassment.

Blushing too, the woman juggles her bag and paperwork in her arms and she puts out her hand. "Hi, my name's Jess. It's very nice to meet you."

Reaching out with his hand, Matthew replies, "Hi, Jess – my name's Matthew. Nice to meet you too." As he shakes her hand, he stares at her perfection. Caught up in the moment, he again blurts out words before thinking: "Would you like to join me and my daughter for a coffee?"

Lucy and Sophie, who have been chattering away as they prepare Matthew's order, suddenly fall silent. The coffee machine screeches away as the boiling hot frothy milk Sophie is holding starts to bubble over, and Lucy stands motionless, the iced bun in her hand hovering above a plate. They both resemble statues.

Jess sends a puzzled look their way.

"Oh, don't worry about the girls," says Matthew. "I'm a regular and – well – in all the years I've been coming here, I've never asked anyone to come and sit with me and my daughter." He starts raising his voice slightly. "*That's* why they're staring…"

Lucy and Sophie jump at Matthew's words.

"Oh, crap," says Lucy under her breath as she drops the iced bun on the floor. Sophie jumps once more as she notices the hot milk frothing over the sides of the metal jug.

"Oh gosh, Lucy, quick, pass me a cloth."

She finally switches off the coffee machine and the two girls kneel on the floor cleaning up the mess they've just made in silence.

Matthew, who a few moments ago was shy and bewildered, has now found his voice. "Please say you'll join us." Presuming she's going to say yes, he asks her, "What can I get you?"

Looking down to the floor in a flirtatious way, Jess begins twisting the ends of her hair; she looks up to Matthew and enchantingly begins to gaze into his eyes, holding his full attention.

"Matthew, thank you for the wonderful invite…"

Waiting patiently for a response, he looks back at her, spellbound. He desires nothing more than to find out who this woman is. With her head held high she accepts his offer.

Internally bouncing up and down like a child with excitement, Matthew asks, "What would you like?"

Looking to the menu above the counter, she says, "Hmm, please may I request a hot chocolate, extra froth and no marshmallows?"

She has a slight look of disgust on her face. "I'm actually not a huge fan of coffee."

"Huh, you don't like coffee, how can you not like coffee?"

"Well, it's quite simple really – there's only one valid reason why I detest coffee and that is… It tastes far too much like coffee."

Immediately she begins to chuckle, and Matthew joins in. Captivated, Matthew begins to question if this is really happening – and if so, if it is possible to magically stumble across such enchanting beauty and find an instant connection whilst spontaneously going out for coffee, then why hadn't life helped him sooner?

He is amazed by this striking woman who has a strong presence, an air of elegance and, as an added bonus, a sense of humour. Granted, no one could replace his wife, but this instant connection seems somewhat similar.

Matthew feels a magnetic pull that's way out of his control. Their eye contact continues. Whatever this powerful presence is, it doesn't scare him – it draws him in.

He's trying to appear cool, but Matthew is now getting more and more nervous by the second. Instead of letting his handsome features and wonderful personality do the talking for him, he's getting out of sync with himself. He leans slightly on the display case where all the wonderful homemade pastries and cakes are perfectly displayed, but almost immediately his elbow slips off the glass pane. Feeling slightly humiliated he tries to compose himself as Jess holds back her laughter.

Lucy and Sophie look on, gently shaking their heads and very subtly rolling their eyes. They exchange knowing looks and smiles. He clearly likes this woman. Much to Matthew's relief, Sophie interrupts the awkward pleasantries: "Take a seat, you two – I'll bring it over to the table."

Jess looks to Sophie and says, "How very kind. Thank you."

"My God. Thank you," Matthew says quietly as he walks away. Sophie mimes, "Stay cool."

Lucy and Sophie watch as he makes his way over to the table. They would both love nothing more than to see him happily sharing creative ideas and planning growth, happiness and a life with another person.

Walking back to the table with Jess proudly by his side, it suddenly dawns on Matthew that while he was caught up in his giddy school boy mentality, he didn't consider Eve. What is she going to think about this? How will she feel about him inviting this woman over to "The Mastermind Corner"? The very same corner he once shared with her mum. After all, this isn't just any table and chairs, or any café; it has meaning, it has purpose – it has memories. The kind of memories you don't want to replace or have fade. With this thought fresh in his mind, Matthew becomes more nervous than before. But it's too late now; they've reached the table, there's no going back.

Matthew has both his hands inside his pockets, fiddling with a tiny piece of fluff to distract himself. Eve sits arched over, leaning with her elbows firmly placed on the table and holding her phone in both her hands. She peers from the corner of her eye at her dad, then looks up fully with a confused expression on her face when she notices the woman standing next to him. Jess puts her bag and paperwork down at the side of the chair. Eve looks expectantly at her dad, who is for the second time today speechless. Eve's facial expression begins to change and, as the silence grows, the energy circulating in the air becomes awkward. Feeling more and more uncomfortable by the second, Matthew still says nothing. Looking at Eve he wipes his head, which is now forming tiny beads of sweat. He finally starts to speak, but before he can say a word, Jess puts out her hand.

"Hi – I'm Jess. Your father has politely asked me to join you for a drink. I do hope this is okay?"

Eve looks blankly at the hand in front of her, then glances to her dad.

"Eve, don't be so rude!" Matthew says sternly.

Eve crosses her arms and stares at Jess. Without any attempt to shake Jess's hand, she says, "As you know, my name's Eve – enjoy your drink."

Eve gets up from her chair and starts to walk out of the café. As she reaches the edge of the table, Matthew puts out his arm to stop her.

"I apologise for my daughter's behaviour, she's normally very pleasant – aren't you, Eve?"

He turns to his daughter, looking at her with complete desperation and confusion.

"Don't apologise for me – apologise for yourself…" Eve snaps.

Matthew frantically tries to work out what Eve's problem is; he's practically begging her with his expression. Eve rolls her eyes, but seems to relent a little.

"A bit of warning that you were inviting a woman to mum's corner may have been nice. You know that thing you always go on about – mutual *respect*?"

Sitting back in her chair, she puts her elbows onto the table once more, and this time she places her head into her hands. Matthew's relieved. Before taking a seat, he pulls out a chair for Jess, who surprisingly enough sits at the table, seemingly unfazed by Eve's attitude. As they sit down, Sophie comes over with a tray filled with hot drinks and cakes, which she places directly in front of Eve. Sophie looks across the table at Eve, who peers through the gaps in her fingers. The pair make eye contact; Sophie smiles. Laying the cups out in front of her elbows, she whispers, "Don't worry, it'll be okay."

Eve takes a deep breath and looks at her dad, then at Jess. Finally, she takes another deep breath in and as she exhales she stands up, straightens her jacket and puts out her hand. "I'm Eve, nice to meet you," she says

Jess begins to smile and shakes her hand. Relieved, Matthew lets out a huge sigh as both Jess and Eve sit back in their seats. Satisfied with the pleasant exchange between the two, he begins passing them their drinks.

In all the commotion and brief excitement, Matthew has forgotten one thing. Because of his slight hearing loss, Matthew doesn't always hear his phone, and so he always has the volume and vibration turned up to the max. Looking embarrassed, Matthew reaches into his silk-lined pocket and takes out his phone; it's flashing like a strobe light in a nightclub. The reminder tells him that he only has thirty minutes left before his meeting. Starting to panic as he presses the screen, Matthew, for probably the third time today, speaks before he thinks. "Jess, I'm so sorry, I've got an urgent meeting and we must leave now or I'll be late." As he gets to his feet he continues, "But please say you'll join us for dinner this evening at our home."

Eve's jaw drops, and her eyes widen as she continues to stare at her dad in disbelief. Matthew's not even aware of Eve's reaction. He patiently waits for a response, the seconds turning into what feels like hours.

Tucking her hair behind her ear, Jess looks to Matthew and locks eyes with him. Cupping the locket around her neck she says, "Are you sure?"

"Yes, of course. Please say you'll join us."

"How can I refuse? Matthew, that would be amazing, thank you."

Eve shoves her chair back with a loud screech as it scrapes across the floor. She pushes past Jess as though she isn't present and doesn't make eye contact with her dad, or Lucy and Sophie behind the counter, who are now casting concerned glances over to the corner. Lucy hurries out after Eve, whilst Sophie continues to serve the customers. Matthew, now unsure of what to do and where to turn, sees Lucy chasing after Eve, and so he chooses to stay with Jess.

They exchange numbers and he says, "I will text you my address shortly, it's on the beachfront. Do you know it?"

"Yes, I've been there once before. From what I recall it's very beautiful and tranquil there, which is perfect. One of my main pleasures in life is not being disturbed by others."

Matthew looks deep into her eyes and becomes captivated, unable to process his thoughts, or even ask questions like *what do you enjoy eating?* He can't explain what is happening to his emotions, or why he is so fixated on this woman. In a desperate attempt to ensure a second meeting, he says, "I'll make sure Eve is on her best behaviour this evening."

Reaching out to Matthew, she places her hand on his arm and says, "Don't worry, I can handle a teenage girl."

Looking down to her hand, Matthew embraces the moment as she touches him. He replies, "Thank you, but it's really not acceptable. You shouldn't be treated like that." With a pained expression on his face he continues, "I will try and explain this evening why Eve is troubled, but this is no excuse for her rude attitude, I know."

Matthew is so wrapped up in this woman's presence, her energy, her aura. He stands like a love-struck dummy, gazing deep into her big brown eyes, totally oblivious to what is going on outside the café.

CHAPTER THREE

The Awkward Silence

Eve stomps fiercely out into the car park. She's furious and hears nothing but her own voice in her mind. *Our home! Really! Mum's home. What's going on with my dad?*

As Lucy catches up to her, Eve shouts, "Sophie said it would be okay!"

Unaware of what happened inside the café, Lucy looks at Eve, confused. Eve has now stopped walking and is standing at the side of the car. Lucy approaches her with caution.

"Eve, what's happened?"

Unable to control the rage building inside her, Eve shouts out and waves her arms in the air. Her outburst is drawing unwanted attention from passers-by, some of whom are shaking their heads in disgust at this young girl screaming aggressively. Youngsters standing across the way are looking over in shock, whispering to one another and pointing. Eve breaks down, her tears falling uncontrollably.

"I'll tell you what's happened." She slowly places one foot in front of the other, moving closer to Lucy, who nervously steps back. Eve points her finger directly in Lucy's face. "Not only has he brought this woman to our table, my mum's table, he's invited her to *our* home!"

Lucy looks taken aback at Eve. Appearing more and more upset by the second, Eve falls to the ground. Rushing to her side, Lucy cradles Eve tight, kissing her gently on the head. She whispers words meant from the heart, "Please calm down, Eve. I don't like seeing you this way and, well, do you not think you might just be overreacting slightly?"

Taking immediate offence, Eve stands up, pushes Lucy away and once again begins shouting. This time, her face turns red with anger, and saliva flies from out of her mouth as she loses control of her actions and emotions.

"Overreacting! Two minutes in her presence and he's forgotten all about my mum…"

Lucy looks stunned. She's never seen Eve this mad. She turns to go, saying, "I'm going to get Matthew."

"Yeah, right! Good luck with that," shouts Eve.

Just then Matthew appears. He takes in Eve's appearance. Her eyes are completely swollen and tears are falling down her face.

"Darling, there you are…"

"Good luck," Lucy says as she passes him on her way back into the café, looking relieved to get away from the drama.

Eve looks at her dad. Pointing her finger once more, Eve says, "Don't you dare try and act concerned about where *I am*."

Trying to calm the situation, but failing miserably, Matthew says, "Eve – please, we really don't have time for this."

With her blood boiling and her head beginning to hurt from all the shouting, Eve no longer has any desire to engage in a conversation with her dad. Wiping her face in frustration, she gets in the car. The energy, the emotions, the atmosphere, is the complete opposite from earlier – and this time, when Matthew gets in, there's no exchanging pleasantries. The doors are slammed, the radio is off and the vibrational energy that's forcing itself from their physical forms becomes present in the car. They are more distant than ever and an awkward silence settles in as they begin to drive away from the café. They're both so wrapped up in their own pain that they don't notice Jess is at the café window, watching them leave.

Jess peers through the gaps between the leaflets and posters stuck on the glass. With a somewhat cagey and proud expression upon her face, her eyes begin to spark. They're lighting up and appear to have an air of secrecy hidden within them. Holding onto the locket around her neck, she begins twiddling it between her fingers. Her expression turns mysterious and satisfied, a deceitful smirk creeping onto her face. As the car slowly moves past the window of the café, her sole attention and focus is on Eve. Her eyes begin to darken, an eerie mist forming spontaneously around her. Jess tilts her head conceitedly as Matthew and Eve go out of sight.

Matthew and Eve are both deep in thought. It's extremely awkward. Neither of them want to upset or hurt the other anymore than they already have, so they both choose to say nothing. As the clock ticks and the silence becomes deafening, the further apart emotionally these two are growing. It seems impossible for either of them to make the first move towards correcting this. Matthew and Eve are very much stuck in this process. Like a Mexican standoff, they've both decided to continue with their protest, shut down, switch off and dismiss one another. With their energy now supressed, you can see the confusion. How did they get to this point? They were fine less than an hour ago and now, you would think these two are strangers.

Eve looks out the window at some birds flying high overhead. They are so free in the sky. Eve visualises her mum's beautiful face in the clouds as she imagines gliding down the side of the huge mountain. She embraces the fall as she's flying free, making her way to the bottom. Suddenly she *hits* the rocks, head first.

She feels content at this image of her death. Eve is filled with rage and has mentally taken ten steps back. Her sole desire is to free herself from this misery she must now call life. With these dark thoughts filling her mind, Eve can't help but conclude that it would be her best solution. At least that way, if she did free herself and commit suicide, she would once again be reunited with her mum.

Matthew pulls into the huge car park at the Honey Productions office. Although he's the boss, he doesn't have a designated space at the front of the building; he firmly believes in equality. He drives round until he eventually finds a space and parks up. Turning off the engine, Matthew looks to Eve.

"You ready?" he says.

Not wanting to give her dad the satisfaction of eye contact, Eve stares out the window. "No – I'm staying here," she says, just loud enough for him to hear.

"What? This meeting was booked with the attendance of us both. Eve, as you know, sometimes life throws things at us but what you have to do is carry on." Leaning across to Eve he continues, "Darling, this is the real world now. Come on, kidda, it's a simple meeting and I promise it won't take long. Just snap out of whatever this is and come in with me." Attempting to lighten the mood he says, "You can see what it's like behind the scenes of the Honey Empire, ready for when you take the reins one day."

"What, the empire you built with *my* mum? I said I'm staying here, end of!"

"Yes, me and *your* mum built this together. We did this for *you*, Evelyn Jade. So that *you* would have the best start and future." Getting no response, Matthew continues, "Oh, Eve, why must you be so stubborn?"

"Stubborn! Just keep the insults coming why don't you, Dad? I said I'm staying here; I don't want to come to your poxy meeting. I don't want to watch *you* with another woman, and I certainly don't want to go in there and smile to a bunch of people I don't care about while you act like everything's okay. Well, it's not *okay*, Dad!"

"Right, well this is what pays the bills, Eve, and your music lessons, and holidays and everything else you want –so I *must* attend this meeting. Like I said before, I won't be long."

Matthew gets out of the car and *slams* the door. He corrects his suit. Heading to the back of the car he grabs his briefcase from the back seat and shuts the car door, this time gently. He sets off across the busy car park towards the building. Once again, Eve removes her gaze from her dad's direction.

Now alone with her thoughts, she reaches for the cream, leather-covered glove compartment and pulls the catch to open it. Rummaging around, she begins lifting the papers at the front. She grabs an old-looking brown leather-backed book. Gazing at it in her hands triggers a memory of a session with her therapist, Josie…

Josie sits in her usual high-back Chesterfield chair. Eve is sat on the L-shaped couch across from her. She feels exhausted. She just has enough oomph to listen to what Josie is saying.

"Eve, it is hugely important to write out your frustration. The pen to paper technique is the best process for everyone when it comes to healing – the idea behind using a pen, instead of typing, is that with every unique movement that your hand makes, you activate cells within your brain and, as these cells activate, your mind is caused to think. You are, in effect, distracting yourself and your mind from the aggression you have built up. Once you have created this distraction, your mind will naturally begin to release the pent-up anger as you write each word. I encourage you, Eve, to always have a pen and paper easily accessible – this will help inspire you to write down any negative thoughts that you are either holding on to or creating within your mind. The best way to think of this technique is as though you are painting the picture that's being held in your mind. The images you see through your sight, and the anger you feel, you can let go of, but instead of painting the picture in a drawing you're painting the picture in words. Words create thoughts."

Eve simply stares numbly as Josie continues, "Eve, it doesn't matter if only you can understand what's written – as long as you are thinking, hearing and releasing the words as you write them, you will begin to free the anger from your mind whilst at the same time letting go of your attachment to this."

Opening the leather-backed book, Eve begins turning the pages, quickly flicking through. The yellow pages fly by one after the other, each one filled with black lines and masses of writing. Every word has been written in scrawling joined writing with blue ink. Without acknowledging the content on the pages, she reaches a blank page. Taking out her blue pen from the glove compartment she writes the following:

"So, today's the day. I knew this would come, the day dad forgets all about you and moves on, like you never existed, like you're not a part of me too. Why should I have to sit and watch him forget that you were ever part of our lives?

If he carries this on, Mum, I promise you, I'm coming. I will join you in the afterlife.

I can't be expected to live a lie while watching him play happy family with another woman. I'm just not strong enough, Mum; you would have known that, so how can Dad not?

Argh, why's Dad being a complete dick? Mum, why did you have to leave us?

I hate myself! Why did you have to go?

Dropping the pen on the page, Eve raises her head to the sky. Getting teary-eyed, she knows her mum isn't coming back and unless she commits suicide and the afterlife is real, she isn't going to be reunited with her anytime soon.

An emotional wreck, Eve's now feeling powerless and broken. She's uncontrollably shedding tears. Each pear-shaped drop contains her pain and these begin to fall down her face, quicker than the rain travels from the sky and hits the ground on a stormy night. Eve's becoming more and more inconsolable by the second. She picks up her pen, looks to the page, which now holds her tears, and writes these four heart-breaking words:

It's all my fault!

Time passes quickly, and soon enough Matthew appears from out of the building. Eve becomes uncomfortable; she doesn't want her dad to see her this way and desperately tries to hide her depression and compose herself. She shoves the book and the pen back into the glove compartment, slamming the door shut. She flicks down the sun visor on the car, slides back the small cover and reveals the tiny hidden mirror. Staring at her pale blotchy face, Eve frantically tries to disguise the redness as she quickly wipes her eyes. Without success, she reaches to the side of the car door and pulls out her huge expensive designer black sunglasses with gold trimming; she places these on her face in a last-ditch attempt to hide her suffering.

With her elbow on the window ledge of the car door again, this time she isn't full of life. She's resting her forehead in the palm of her hand, hiding her inner expression of sheer hopelessness. Eve would love nothing more than for her mum to appear magically.

Matthew gets in the car and endeavours to make conversation with Eve. "Evelyn Jade Honey – please speak to me," he says, his voice low. Looking across at his daughter with an expression of complete despair and helplessness, he continues, "Why did you react that way in the café?"

Eve is still withdrawn and not ready to speak. She continues to look out of the window.

"I can't help you if you don't open up to me…"

Eve's still listening to her inner voice.

Don't fall for it, Eve, he's trying to sweet talk you. Remember, he didn't chase after you at the café. No, he stayed with her. You're right, he's wrong, don't answer him.

The voice in Eve's mind is getting louder and louder as she tunes in and receives the words it's feeding her. Choosing to take the advice, Eve remains withdrawn.

Matthew once again attempts to speak to his daughter. "Darling, please – you should know there isn't a woman in the universe who could replace your mum. I ask you, Evelyn Jade, can I not have a female friend?"

Still Matthew receives no response from Eve. He begins to sigh as he looks down at the floor of the car, his head now hanging low and heavy. Matthew doesn't want to give up, but he also doesn't know what to do, or where to turn. What he is clear on is that his daughter is seriously unhappy at the thought of him potentially becoming happy. Is he supposed to be alone forever? Matthew starts the car. Reaching out to put it into first gear, he looks up as small raindrops begin to hit the windscreen one after the other. The sky suddenly becomes overcast and dark. He looks to his left with sorrow deep in his eyes, the same eyes which this morning were filled with life and love as he was sharing precious moments with his blessing, his best friend, his Eve. He can't help but feel an overwhelming surge of inner sadness. No more smiles, no more laughter. She's staring out the window and no longer acknowledging his existence.

Eve hasn't moved an inch since he entered the car. With her sunglasses on she appears to be looking into a dark abyss, deep in thought. Matthew notices a tear roll down her cheek, which she quickly wipes away.

What should he do? He really hasn't got a clue. Reversing out of the parking space, Matthew prays the answers will be shown to him.

CHAPTER FOUR

The Arrival

Matthew is in his airy, brand-new, bright white painted kitchen, surrounded by pots and pans. He's dressed in relaxed casual clothes under his macho pinafore. He's got the radio on and is dancing away in what can only be described as an embarrassing dad-like fashion. He's immensely happy, even after the day's events. He's completely enjoying the moment alone. He's decided he's putting all his energy into this evening; he's confident Eve will snap out of her mood soon. He's getting excited at the thought of actually having a date, after being alone for so long.

Making his way over to the fridge, he grabs the grey metal tray containing four large seasoned raw chicken breasts. Reaching into the drawer at the side of the fridge, he pulls out his white latex gloves. Pulling these onto his hands, he sets about dicing the chicken on the red meat chopping board. The oven is preheating and the accompanying ingredients have also been diced and are lying neatly on the black marble surface top of the grey kitchen island. Matthew's suffers from obsessive compulsive disorder (OCD); this means everything must be colour coded and have its own place. The red peppers have been chopped with precision and perfection and are organised into a neat little pile, as are the green peppers, mushrooms, herb-coated new potatoes and red onions. Grabbing a frying pan from the oversized matte black hanging pot rack above his head, he makes his way over to the huge modern built-in black Range cooker and begins frying the chicken. His thoughts begin to drift; he wonders how this evening is going to progress. Will it get worse, will it get better, will they discover family life is again complete and live in blissful harmony? Who knows…?

The radio is still blaring and Matthew starts to shake his extremely toned butt, dancing and singing along, showing his best Salt and Pepa tribute routine to the chicken in the frying pan.

Eve sits in her bedroom in complete silence. She has decided that she's taking no part in the charade her dad is creating downstairs. The room is bright, clean and filled with all her favourite things. The walls are the same as every wall in the house, painted only with the purest white. The only colour present within the room is on the curtains that hang off the pole, her floral bedsheets and the small heart-shaped mosaic of photographs she's created over her bed, made up of photos of her and her mum. There is also a small en-suite in her room which contains a shower cubicle, toilet and a small white ceramic sink with a mirror above it, also in the shape of a heart. Next to the en-suite is a balcony that overlooks the sea.

Sat on her neatly made bed wearing her ripped jeans and grey casual t-shirt, Eve holds a scruffy-looking brown teddy bear tightly to her chest. He has a grubby red and white polka dot bow-tie around his neck. It's obvious that this delicate bear has been smothered with love by the signs of wear and tear on his fluffy body. Half of his right ear is missing and there is stuffing sticking out of his black button eyes. This is one of her most cherished possessions. The bear she holds so tightly and smothers with love was her mum's. His name is Gregg. This bear knew her mum longer than any of them; he was a gift from *her* grandmother when she was born. Her mum treasured Gregg always, and when Eve was a child, she would never let her play with the delicate bear for fear that he would fall apart. When her mum died, Eve and her dad were sorting through her mum's possessions when Eve found Gregg tucked away in a shoebox, wrapped in gold tissue paper. As she lifted him out, she saw his features; they were a true reflection of her emotions. With Gregg in her hands looking sad, lost and lonely, she couldn't help it. Immediately she broke down crying. Gregg had lost his owner too. Eve has kept him close ever since. She now has her own personal strong connection with Gregg, just like her mum. Looking into his deep black button eyes, she says, "I never meant for any of this to happen."

Lauren Honey didn't die due to Mother Nature, she wasn't struck down with an illness, it wasn't a long process that everyone's mind could get used to before the inevitable happened. Lauren was in fact *killed*.

The doorbell rings loudly. Matthew looks at his watch and sees it is 7.30. He walks out of the kitchen, slicking the sides of his hair back with both his hands. He appears to be in a slight fluster; his palms are sweating, and he gives himself a pep talk as he makes his way to the door.

"Just be yourself, Matthew. Just be yourself."

At the bottom of the stairs, next to the front door, there's a grand floor-length mirror with a thick gold frame. Lauren chose the majority of the decor in the house; this item was her favourite. She had a very keen eye for interior design and she loved how this particular mirror opened up the doorway.

He takes a moment to check himself out in the mirror. He has dressed to impress in his dark denim designer jeans, navy-blue shirt and deep navy-blue blazer jacket. As he straightens himself up, he can't help but look at his reflection and see the truth: he may be externally oozing confidence, but internally he's apprehensive and nervous. He's still confused and struggling to work out what's so captivating about this woman. He can't help himself; Matthew feels like a teenager all over again, with butterflies in his stomach and hope in his heart. Hope that destiny and fate may not have forgotten about him after all. He understands and accepts that he will never have another soul mate – you only get one. But sometimes he gets lonely and longs for that wonderful adult connection. He knows Eve will one day grow and live a blessed life with another, and rightly so: this is what he desires for her to have, a life of freedom.

So, what would be left for him? Matthew would love to be able to share his journey with another person again; is this her? Before he knows it, he's answering the door.

Outside darkness is gently beginning to fall. Standing on the doorstep gazing back at Matthew with smiles on their faces and bright beady eyes are two Jehovah's Witnesses. They're both wearing matching black and white suits. He can see the thick black straps hanging over their shoulders from the backpacks on their backs. They both have similar short, neat hairstyles. Matthew notices that not only is their appearance strangely mirroring one another's, like identical twins, but they both appear to be holding the same items in the same manner in their hands. Each one holds a Bible in one hand and a chunk of leaflets in the other. One of the friendly looking gents speaks up. "Sir, do you have a moment to talk about our Lord, Christ the saviour?" he says in a confident and loud tone.

"Erm, sorry lads, I'm a bit busy right now."

"We promise, sir, we'll only take a moment of your t—"

Before he finishes his sentence the two men *freeze*. Perfectly in sync with each other, they release the silky leaflets they are holding, letting them drop on the floor. Again, in sync with each other, they cling to their Bibles, holding them tightly with both hands.

Moving his head back slightly, Matthew looks on, confused, at this random unexpected action. Both the Jehovah's Witnesses now have their eyelids wide open. It looks as though their eyes are beginning to protrude from out of their sockets. Without any explanation, they slowly start to walk backwards and in an almost robotic-sounding manner, the Jehovah's Witness who hasn't yet spoken says, "We're sorry to disturb you, sir. You have a pleasant, erm, evening now."

With their smart, immaculate black shoes, they begin placing one foot behind the other and continue to walk *slowly* backwards. The pair, still clinging to their Bibles, do not make any attempt to turn around. Without breaking eye contact with Matthew, they vanish into thin air.

"You forgot your leaflets." Bending down to pick them up, he shakes his head. "That was weird…"

He looks at the leaflets; they're pale blue with a picture of the clearest sky. Spread out in the middle of the clouds, in white bold font, is a slogan that reads: "Why you can trust the bible: One man died for us all." Standing strong and proud towards the bottom of the leaflet is a white cross. Matthew stares out into the garden. Stepping backwards into the house, as he reaches to shut the door, he looks up and sees an outline approaching him. Assuming it's one of the Jehovah's Witnesses returning for their leaflets, he says, "Ah, here you go, gents." But he gets no reply.

Confused, he looks more closely at the outline that's making its way towards him. He can see a single figure. It's Jess. She's standing tall and making her way up the path with a smile on her face. Her lips are painted red and her long dark-brown hair is beautifully styled and blowing in the breeze. She looks glamourous, wearing a tight-fitted red dress which sits perfectly around her waist and hips. The material is hugging her figure with perfection. This woman oozes a provocative energy; Matthew is captivated. There isn't anything at this point that could stop this man from falling in immediate love with this woman; like a love-struck boy, he's hooked.

As he locks eyes with Jess, he's speechless. Her eye colour is the deepest shade of brown, but when she looks at him they become so intense, they spark and almost look as though they're turning an enticing shade of black. Matthew is mesmerised. Jess stands looking back at Matthew in an extremely flirtatious manner. For the second time today, he is staring at her.

"Good evening, Matthew."

The only word his mind can process is, "Hi…"

Looking confident and satisfied with his reaction to her presence, she immediately responds, "Well – are you going to invite me in, or are we eating outside?"

"S-sorry, erm, yes, p-please, come in," Matthew replies, finally snapping out of his trance.

Clutching a sliver clasp bag and wearing strappy silver three-inch stiletto heels, she places one foot in front of the other, strutting her stuff as she enters the house. Her walk is captivating.

"Eve has decided she won't be joining us this evening," Matthew says as he closes the door.

"Don't worry, I'm sure she's seen enough of me for one day," Jess replies, not looking too concerned.

Matthew looks embarrassed. "Honestly, she really is a beautiful girl inside and out. I know you two would really get on," he says.

Jess says nothing, looking at him with a whatever-you-say kind of expression.

"She's never rude to anyone – actually, I haven't seen her like that before. Even after everything we've been through, she's never been that rude to another person."

Jess starts to laugh. "Should I feel honoured, then?"

Matthew decides it's best to get off the subject of Eve. He invites Jess into the dining room.

"Would you like a glass of wine?" Then, remembering her comment about coffee earlier, he smiles and adds, "Or does it taste too much like wine?"

"Wine would be great. Thank you."

Realising his joke has fallen flat, Matthew awkwardly laughs. He then goes to the kitchen and returns with a bottle of rosé.

"My favourite wine. Have you been secretly spying on me, Mr Honey?"

Blushing at this coincidence, he replies, "No, I only stalk people on the weekend."

There is a sudden bang. Matthew and Jess look up at the dining room door.

"Eve!" Matthew shouts. There's no reply.

Excusing himself, he heads to the front door. He opens it and shouts once again, "Eve…" Still, he gets nothing back.

Matthew stands on the cold grey step outside the door, wearing nothing but his black socks on his feet. He hears the sound of waves gently crashing onto the beach one after the other. The tide's now coming in and the scent of salty water is in the air. Looking out, Matthew can't see a single person.

Eve is already halfway down the street. Marching down the pathway at a speedy pace, she's made her decision: she doesn't like this woman and can't explain why, all she knows is something just doesn't feel right. Eve has absolutely no desire to be in Jess's presence. Even as the darkness engulfs her small frame, she doesn't care. She's on a mission and nothing is going to get in her way.

When her mum died, to occupy her mind and bring a sense of meaning to her life, Eve created "Lauren's Garden of Secrets" so she would always have somewhere to go and be alone with her thoughts and her mum. Each time she heads here with just one intention – to feel her mum's presence and speak to her whilst also, if required, letting off some steam. Eve asks for guidance, help, love and support from the spiritual world surrounding her, with belief and faith that it's her mum's spiritual influence. This healing process may not be for everyone and sometimes passers-by look at her like she's insane as she moves around in frustration, trying desperately to gain some form of understanding. She doesn't always receive the answers she wants, but this process helps her walk away with some form of clarity. Eve knows that after today's events and what is currently going on in the house, "Lauren's Garden of Secrets" is the only place she wants to be, and so that is where she is heading at full speed.

The street lights are shining brightly and as she passes directly under them they light up her face. She's bright red, huffing, puffing and out of breath. She's wearing her light denim ripped jeans, black school leavers hoodie and her hiking trainers, with her backpack hanging low off her shoulders. It's tatty brown suede with brightly coloured badges sown on the side.

Ideally, Eve doesn't want to return to the house until Jess has left, but she knows she must be home no later than 10 p.m. Gripping the straps of her backpack with both hands, Eve suddenly fills with intense anger and aggression. Unable to hold the words in any longer, she begins talking to herself out loud: "Why is Dad putting me in this position? I don't understand. Was I not loud enough? I showed him. I am not ready to deal with the replacement of Mum. Why is he ignoring this?"

Still without answers, Eve takes a deep breath in and slowly begins counting back from five. She calms slightly, becoming less irritated with every inch she gets further away from home and closer to her destination. Eve looks to the sky and speaks to the stars, questioning the universe: "Is this how it's supposed to be? Am I supposed to sit back and watch my dad forget all about my mum – and then what, just move on like she never existed? Am I expected to play happy family with another woman? Oh, hello step-mum, yes, my day's been amazing, what about yours? Yeah, right, like I care, just saying it doesn't feel right! Why are you doing this to me?"

Puzzled, alone and running out of energy, Eve feels her aggression begin to subside as her head throbs. Feeling a deep inner sense of grief, Eve continues speaking out loud: "I've just lost one parent; do I really have to go through it all again? I've just started to have a *normal* relationship with my dad. A real father-daughter relationship. You should know I've not had that since I was little. I ask you, universe – have you given him his wish? Is my dad truly going to risk losing me for a woman he's just met?"

Eve slows down as she mulls over this question. Staring down at the street, she places one foot in front of the other. Her mind begins projecting a memory through the windows of her eyes.

Eve sees her dad. He's a broken man. He sits on a brown mahogany bench, wearing a black suit with a small artificial sunflower tucked in the pocket on the front of his jacket. It's her mum's funeral.

Her dad is sobbing uncontrollably. Reaching out, Eve holds him tightly in her arms, placing his head close to her heart. She's wearing the silver chain and heart-shaped locket round her neck. Eve rests her chin in her dad's hair as tears roll down her face.

In the huge church with its extravagant multi-coloured stained-glass windows, Eve is surrounded by relatives and loved ones. She's in complete disbelief and shock at the harsh reality that it's her precious mum lying lifeless in the box in front of her. Unable to control her emotions anymore and unable to console this broken man in her arms, she releases him and runs over to the coffin.

Eve's expression is pained – she almost looks nothing like herself, she is that exhausted. She has allowed her emotions to take full control. Before she has time to process her actions, she heads towards the coffin with tears streaming from her eyes and fluid uncontrollably gushing from her nose. Her face is swollen. Eve can barely see the floor beneath her feet, let alone what's in front of her. But what she can see, as clear as the daylight outside, is the white coffin that holds her mum's lifeless body. In utter desperation and not wanting to accept the reality, she kicks out and screeches, "Noooooooo…"

The white wooden coffin is at the centre of the ceremony, the main focus of the church, standing strong on the platform. It's surrounded by beautiful, bright sunflowers that beam radiantly like the sun in all its glory. Yellow and orange luminous bouquets share their natural glow, creating a warm, angelic vision. And yet, the energy, the mood, the vibration is the complete opposite. Approaching the platform, Eve reaches out in her desperate attempt to grab the coffin. Suddenly, Eve is stopped and forcefully turned around. She sees it's her mum's twin sister, her Auntie Christina. She's wearing black from head to toe and has a black netted veil draped over her face. She holds Eve tightly in an attempt to console this young vulnerable soul, whispering in Eve's ear, "Ssshhhhhhh…"

They collapse onto the floor, and Christina whispers once more into Eve's ear, "Shhh… My child, my precious Eve, I know your pain – she was once my only best friend too."

With these words, Eve crumbles. She starts rocking back and forth. She's inconsolable and begins screaming out in pain, "Why? Please come back to me. I'm sorry! Mum… I said I'm sorry – I never meant for this to happen… Please God, take me instead."

Quickly shaking this vision out of her head, Eve comes back to reality. She continues to march down the streets, wiping the tears off her face as she proceeds with her mission. Walking at an even faster pace, her breath gets quicker and quicker as her heartrate increases.

Eve feels a wrench in her stomach as her mind brings up another memory, this time of her dad.

They're at home in the day room. Matthew sits on the brown cosy couch with a glass of red wine in his hand, beige decorative cushions either side. He's talking away to Eve, as she's sat on the floor, but this time he has happiness in his features and a smile on his face. They are surrounded by pictures and boxes overflowing with old photographs. The boxes smell damp and have scuffs on the edges where they've been banged about and stored away for years, transferred from home to home.

The room is warm and cosy as the fire flickers, spreading its natural glow. Matthew almost spills his red wine in his excitement as he shares stories of the adventures he enjoyed with her mum. The photographs are endless. So many memories and so many wonderful times. Her dad is joyful and smiling as he relives the moment in each picture, for its uniqueness, as though it was happening today. This makes her genuinely smile.

Eve looks at the ground as the memory fades. Why is her dad willing to risk losing what they have built for some woman he's known for a matter of hours? Eve's unable to answer this. Her heart rate has speeded up and she's completely out of breath and at the same time relieved as she finally arrives at her destination, "Lauren's Garden of Secrets".

A simple wooden bench stands strong, beautifully positioned at the top of a cliff. The scene is simple, yet stunning. Eve can just about make out the outline of the sandy cliffs that surround the beach. The sun has long since dipped below the horizon, but she is still able to observe the beauty of the ocean. Closing her eyes, Eve can hear the waves as they gently bring the tide in. Breathing deeply, she can taste the salt in the air.

Eve never struggled to embrace the beauty of nature when she was younger. She knew she was blessed, she knew the importance of life. But now she struggles to feel and embrace any part of her existence. Eve understood she was extremely lucky to have both her parents together. Not only did they remain together, they still shared love for one another, as strong as the day they first met. A functioning, joyous, solid family unit and a true place to call home. She had friends that weren't so fortunate. Fate had different plans for their upbringing and most of them grew up in broken homes. They always adapted well; it was a normal way of life for them. They accepted that their parents didn't like each other, and it didn't faze them. Of course they would have loved nothing more than to live a life with Mum and Dad, at least that way they wouldn't have to deal with the messy bits in between, but they couldn't change things.

Eve would see her friends leave and spend the odd weekend with Dad, while living with Mum. Some, although it was rare, would live the opposite way around, staying with Dad and spending the weekend with Mum.

When her mum died, Eve shut out all her friends. She felt they didn't appreciate how different her circumstances were to theirs. How could they even begin to compare to what she must deal with? She would often get annoyed and shout to her friends, "It is *not* the same!", as they would try and sympathise with her.

Okay, yes, Eve has a broken home – yes, she is no longer part of the two-parent family, but it isn't through her parents choosing to separate. They didn't have a huge falling out and the main point of all this is she doesn't have the opportunity to see both her parents – they do.

Eve, a young girl who once embraced life, felt blessed and was filled with gratitude, quickly slipped. Now she feels cursed and bitter.

Sitting quietly on the bench, Eve inhales the pure air and looks out at the outlines of the cliffs surrounding her. The night is inked in darkness.

Eve places her backpack next to her on the bench and opens it. She takes out her number-one treasured possession: a picture of her and her mum. At least once every two months they would dedicate a day to spend time together, doing anything they both enjoyed. The jam-packed action days would range from paint balling and theme parks to spa days and fashion shows. Eve took this selfie on their last ever mum and daughter day at their favourite spa and restaurant. It was *exactly* two weeks before her mum died.

Eve's innocent, vibrant, life-fuelled face smiles out of the photo, her hair bright, long and shiny. In the background, her mum sits up high on a black leather massage bed. Her dark chocolate long hair, which is styled to perfection, is draped over her shoulders and is complemented by the white fluffy robe she's wearing. And, of course, *no* spa outfit would be complete without matching slippers. She's holding a glass of champagne in her left hand.

Eve can't help but grin at the sight of her mum's beautiful white beaming smile. It's so full of life, full of hope and radiating love. But her smile soon fades as an overwhelming surge of sadness takes over at the loss of this beautiful woman, mother and soul.

Also inside the backpack is the bow-tied teddy bear, Gregg, along with Eve's diary and a blue pen. Holding this tightly in her hand she gazes up at the sky. The stars align and begin to glisten gently in the distance. The universe is such a beautiful place. All Eve sees is freedom. Speaking to the brightest star she can find she says, "Which one are you? Hmm, I know – the one that shines the brightest, that's you, Mum."

Looking down at her mum's beautiful face in the picture she smiles as a tear falls on the glass that protects the image. She's been to "Lauren's Garden of Secrets" more times than she can count in the past three years. Feeling cursed and suicidal, sometimes all she wanted to do was run and jump off the edge of the cliff.

Closing her eyes, she begins to visualise her surroundings, but in daylight. In her mind's eye she's sitting on the bench with the tatty brown suede backpack on the ground next to her. Suddenly, she stands. Holding the picture tightly in her hand and without a single tear on her face, Eve walks to the edge of the cliff. She curiously leans over the side, looking down. The drop is at least one thousand feet. There are rocks scattered all the way down and a huge pile of them at the bottom.

Becoming extremely intrigued as she peers over, Eve looks deeper and deeper as an abyss of darkness forms in her mind. She heads back to the bench, but then unexpectedly turns and, without so much as a second thought, quickly runs towards the edge. As she takes her last steps, there is a smile on her face, and as her feet clear the edge, Eve's shouting, "I'm coming for you, Mum!"

Reaching up to grab the clouds in the bright blue sky, she hasn't felt this free for so long. She's done it, she's over the edge and totally unfazed by the irreversible consequences of this action. Now diving head first with her arms like wings, the picture of her and her mum still in her hand, gliding like a bird, Eve's finally free. Free from the life she'd been forced to learn to live. Smiling, laughing and embracing the air as it hits her face, Eve gracefully glides down this magnificent cliff, accepting each second as the breeze gently kisses her face.

But just before she hits the rocks at the bottom, she releases her mind from the visualisation process and opens her eyes. She's still sat on the bench. She isn't over the edge and it isn't daylight. Looking down at the picture in her hand, Eve feels sadness and sorrow. The only thing that has ever stopped her from committing suicide is the unknown impact on her dad. Surely, he would suffer even more. Unanswerable questions begin racing in her mind.

How will Dad cope? How will Dad deal with not only losing his wife, but losing the only person in his life who has a connection to her, me?

Eve cares so much about her dad she chooses not to kill herself. Although she closes her eyes from time to time and visualises the run and jump, embracing how free she feels in her mind as her body makes its way down to the ground, this is nothing more than a thought. A sense of freedom when she's completely trapped in an existence she just wants to run away from.

CHAPTER FIVE

What Happened?

Matthew isn't worried about Eve. He's been here so many times before, when Eve's stormed out of the house, and he knows she will come back home no later than her curfew time. His homemade specialty is thickening in the oven and the fragrance of chicken and casserole juices can be smelt throughout the whole house, making it feel cosy, warm and once again like a family home. Matthew and Jess are in the dining room, surrounded by walls painted the purest white. The only colour present in the room is on the expensive, thick gold curtains hanging heavy either side of the double doors that lead to just one of the many balconies overlooking the crisp English sea. An extravagant diamond chandelier hangs from the ceiling at the perfect centre of the room, refracting specks of light that glow like stars on the walls.

They sit at the luxurious solid wooden table, which is surrounded by six high-back, expensive, black-leather chairs. At the centre of the table sits an old-fashioned white-lace cotton doily, on which stands a vintage, solid silver candle holder. The exquisite vintage piece holds a pure-white unlit candle in each of its six arms. Matthew and Jess's wine glasses sit on black and gold mats. The rest of the table is bare.

The minimalism is attributed to Matthew's OCD, which he has developed since losing his wife. He can't bear to have too many items laid out and surrounding him. His mind becomes confused and torturous as it feeds him words of destruction over the untidiness before his eyes. Often, Matthew struggles when he finds himself visiting family or at other people's homes. If there are a lot of dissimilar items out in front of him placed in an unorganised fashion, his mind goes into overdrive, desiring nothing more than to place every item in a precise order. More recently, he has started to move items around until he is content and satisfied with their positioning. Most people no longer question this and simply leave him to it. It's an ongoing psychological battle that only Matthew himself can conquer, but at least when he's at home he can stay calm as nothing leans so much as a centimetre out of place.

Caught up in the moment and appreciating each other's company, Matthew and Jess laugh as they discuss how embarrassing their initial meeting was today at the café.

"Oh, Matthew, don't be so hard on yourself. I thought your response was cute, and I must admit I was very flattered. Personally, I think you are a very handsome man, and also, may I say, your style, Matthew, is exquisite. There is no greater attraction to me than a man who has his own style."

"You're making me blush, but thank you – and, well, I beg to differ. Honestly, I don't know what came over me, I couldn't speak. I felt a right daft git. I could only imagine what you were thinking."

The wine is flowing and the evening progressing well, so Matthew is taken unawares by Jess's next question.

"Matthew, if you don't mind me asking – what happened with you and Eve's mum?"

After the events that had taken place today and Eve's continued protest, he knew this question would be asked at some point – but he truly didn't expect to be answering it so soon. Closing his eyes if only for a brief second, Matthew takes a deep breath in, almost filling his lungs, then, as he exhales he opens his eyes. Jess is looking directly at him from across the table with a captivating expression, encouraging him to speak. She reaches under the table and holds onto his thigh with a firm grip.

Somehow gathering his strength, he begins to explain: "I met Lauren, Eve's mum, in my late twenties. We were both young and travelling around the world. We didn't know each other and yet we both set out on the same adventure, at the same time, with the same intention. We both wanted to take time out from education and work to embrace everything the world had to offer, including all the different cultures." Trying to remain strong, Matthew continues, "Not too far into our individual trips we both ended up staying in the same hostel in Thailand. It was fate that brought us together. Lauren was travelling alone, as was I – we were a pair of loners and loved it. I'm not sure if you know this, but when you're travelling, you stay in hostels, and more often than not you get mixed or single-sex dorms. I always chose the single-sex dorm, as did Lauren, but this hostel was fully booked and we had to sleep in the mixed dorm. I was on the top bunk when Lauren arrived. I saw her huge smile from the corner of my eye as soon as she appeared in the room; her natural beauty completely blew me away. I remember lifting my head out of the book I was reading and just looking over like, wow, who is she? Instantly, we became best friends. Honestly, I've *never* had so much in common with anyone, let alone a woman. Every day was a brand-new adventure, we had so much fun together. I knew, within a matter of seconds, that Lauren was my soul mate. A bold statement to make, but I just couldn't ignore the intense connection, it was super powerful. It was too strong for either of us to pull away, and actually, we didn't want to. We both decided to take a huge leap of faith – with multiple countries left to visit, we made a decision to only visit places that we'd never been to before. We spent the rest of our travelling days together. It was great and exceeded our wildest dreams.

"When I set off travelling I had absolutely *no* idea I would meet my future wife. My intention was to be free and to see the world – and yet fate had different plans for me."

Matthew stops speaking. He realises who he is actually having this conversation with. It's not a friend, or a family member, it's a woman he's only just met today. Does she really want to hear him declaring his love for his now deceased wife?

"Sorry – I didn't realise, I'm getting carried away with myself."

"No, please, continue – you loved Lauren dearly. It shows your vulnerable and sensitive side, and to me, Matthew, that just proves you are a man of integrity."

"Thank you, I think. I suppose sometimes I feel blessed to have found her and to have been able to share a section of my life with a woman who was so beautiful, inside and out. And yet, at the same time, it's like a cruel curse. Maybe you're right, I am slightly sensitive, but I'm still here and, well..."

Matthew stares into Jess's eyes from across the table. Standing, he makes his way around the chairs. Sitting down next to Jess, he leans in and tucks her hair behind her ear. Unable to hold the words in any longer he says, "You are so beautiful."

Jess smiles. "You're too kind. But thank you."

"What is it... I mean – why am I so drawn to you?"

"Well, I'm not sure what *it* is that you are specifically referring to, but please, continue with your story..."

Coughing, with a slight hint of embarrassment at his apparent rejection, he replies, "Yes, of course, sorry, I got slightly side-tracked, where was I?"

"You were describing how you decided to travel together, and how fate had different plans for you both. I have a question, Matthew, do you truly believe in fate?"

"Yes, I mean, most definitely. Fate is your life – and no matter how you try, you can never change it. Unfortunate or not, the cards you are dealt are the cards you must live with. I have visualised going back so many times to see if I could have changed my fate, changed what happened, and changed the tragic circumstance I now feel forced to live, and each time, there is nothing. Each time, I could say maybe this, or maybe that, but the facts are, if I went back it would all happen the exact same way. So why would I wish to go through such traumatic events all over again? Look at it this way – it was actually fate that I met you. I had an important meeting this afternoon. It was to be Eve's first time attending an appointment with me as my assistant. She was so nervous, I could tell. We shared a moment this morning, thinking about Lauren, and so, to distract her and relieve some of the pressure, I suggested that we go to the café. Okay, so she didn't attend the meeting, and things took an unexpected turn, but I wouldn't have met you if I didn't make that choice. You see, it was fate that I should be there to meet you."

"Your perception of fate is extremely interesting. I guess your acceptance of this is what drew me to your family. Sorry – now I'm side-tracking, please continue…"

"Why'd you ask?"

"No reason, really – well, other than I have actually been waiting a long time for a family dynamic such as this. Now that I have you… let's just say, time will tell. After all, like you say, you cannot change your fate."

Matthew is slightly confused by Jess's choice of words, but she seems somewhat eccentric, so he chooses to refrain from digging into what she means by this.

"Please, Matthew, continue, I'm enjoying hearing your story."

"Erm, okay, yeah, sure, well… I think I understand what you mean. Would you like me to continue with how I met Lauren, or do you want me to skip to what happened?"

"I am enjoying watching your face light up as you speak about her. I'm sure you will explain what happened to Lauren in your own time."

Matthew smiles as he continues, "You're such a unique woman. This is always very hard for me and I truly appreciate your compassion and understanding."

"Thank you. I'm happy that you are able to be so open with me about such a sensitive subject."

"You just seem different. I feel as if I already know you, but I don't. I can't explain it, well, other than somehow it doesn't seem awkward telling you this. It's like you already know what I'm about to say. I don't know. It's all very confusing. I mean, take for instance this. When we were travelling, we came across an old gypsy lady's stall. She was selling jewellery. Lauren instantly fell in love with a solid silver locket. It had a tiny little angel on it and was hanging from a delicate silver chain. I bought it when she wasn't looking and gave it to her that same night as the sun was setting. It was my special token of thanks to her for lighting up my life. Lauren never took it off and, well, since she, you know, passed, Eve has worn the necklace and she's never once taken it off. The necklace is very similar, if not identical, to the one you wear around your neck. Except, on your locket, your angel isn't smiling."

"Really? What a coincidence."

"Yes, and if I truly look into your eyes, and I mean deeply enough, it's as though I can see Lauren. Like she lives on through you. I'm probably freaking you out now, aren't I? See, I would never think about saying these things to anyone, *ever*, let alone a woman I've just met."

Jess smiles and says, "I'm here now. Maybe it's a good thing I remind you of Lauren. Everything happens for a reason. You agree with me, right?"

"Yes."

"So, we're both in agreement that this, right now, is potentially happening for a reason?"

"Yes. Why'd you ask?"

"I, too, have been alone for a long time. I, too, have been wandering the universe lost, waiting for the right soul. Matthew Honey, we have been placed together for intentions that are yet to appear in our lives. I'm intrigued. Although you may think I know what happened to Lauren, I actually know nothing."

Matthew sighs deeply; his expression changes. Dread, fear and gut-wrenching pain are plastered across his face. Jess moves closer to him. Placing her hand on his shoulder, she gently rests her chin on top of her hand and quietly says directly into his ear, "Matthew, what happened to your wife, what happened to Lauren?"

Closing his eyes, Matthew takes a deep breath in and as he exhales he slowly opens his eyes and begins, "It was just after six, evening time, over three years ago now. On the seventh of July. I'll never forget it, the date haunts me – I remember it too well. The day surfaces in my mind at least once a day, every day, since it happened. Lauren and I had collected Eve from her music lesson."

Matthew looks to the floor. He's struggling to hide his sorrow, less eager now to speak. This is his least favourite subject. Nonetheless, holding back his tears and regaining his strength, Matthew continues,

"We would always collect Eve from her tutor's home together. It was the same routine every Wednesday and practically like clockwork. Pretty much every step was taken at the same time every week. Anyone who was watching us would be able to predict our arrival time, it was that regular." He laughs slightly as he realises how fixed his routine used to be.

Coughing and attempting to resume his composure he continues, "We were making our way back towards the shops where we parked the car. Eve was telling us about the solo she had just learned."

Suddenly he lets out the biggest sigh.

"My phone began to ring – you've heard how loud it is – and so I stopped to take the call. I was standing still in the street, concentrating on the call. There was a problem at work. One of the clients was requesting changes to the rough edit we sent across. Just as I was asking them to send confirmation of the changes to me via email, I looked up and could see Eve and Lauren had both carried on walking back to where the car was parked. It was still light-ish outside. Eve was full of life, chatting away."

With this image at the forefront of his mind, it's almost too much for Matthew to bear, as only he knows what's coming next. He raises his hand and presses his thumb and two fingers into his eye sockets to deflect the tears that are about to fall down his face at any given moment.

Jess places her hand onto his leg. Matthew stays still for a brief minute, his face turning a deep shade of red as he holds on tightly to his emotions. He's struggling to speak, trapped in the moment visualising random snapshots of that dreadful evening; he hears the screeching of car tyres and Lauren's desperate scream over and over. He sees the fear on Lauren's face as she watches her baby stand in the middle of the road like a statue. Squeezing his eyes tight and shaking his head, Matthew tries desperately to remove the visions and the noises from his mind.

Once ready, he bravely removes his hand from his face, clears his throat and speaks: "I'd turned my back for a millisecond – the next thing, as I turned my head, I heard Lauren scream Eve's name at the top of her voice. I'm partially deaf in one ear and this was the loudest scream I've ever heard. I felt the vibration ringing through my ears. I lie in bed at night and sometimes I hear the echo of that scream, as though it was uttered only a few seconds ago. Lauren's desperate plea haunts me.

"Eve had walked out into the road without looking. A car suddenly appeared and was heading towards her at high speed. Eve was stood completely frozen in the road." A huge lump forms in Matthew's throat and his voice changes slightly as he continues, "My wife – my soulmate – my beautiful Lauren, being the hero and the amazing mum she'd always been, ran into the road without a thought or a care for her own safety. She grabbed Eve and instantly threw her out of the way."

Matthew slumps, his eyes to the floor, reliving the moment in silence, a broken man. Aware there's now no going back, he clears his throat once more, desperately attempting to be stronger than before. "Lauren was hit by the car with such force it snapped pretty much every bone in her body – as she came crashing down and hit the ground her skull cracked, causing brain damage, and the amount of blood lost resulted in instant death. All I could do was stand by and watch as this happened. It was like my life had developed into a slow-motion movie scene. I could see the look on Lauren's face as she flew into the air. The car hit her legs with such a forceful impact, in milliseconds it had thrown her up onto the bonnet with the biggest bang – it was unbearably loud. By this point, Lauren wasn't even screaming, it was as though she had accepted her fate. She hit the windscreen, and I still hear the crack in my mind as it breaks into a thousand pieces. Her body was thrown up into the sky. Immediately, my body went into shock, and I *couldn't* move. All I could do was stand still, in total disbelief at what my eyes were witnessing. I did nothing to save my daughter or my wife."

Matthew's expression becomes numb and almost trance-like as tears begin to fall rapidly down his face. His expression motionless, he continues, "The immediate blow threw Lauren so high into the air my heart broke instantly. I knew she wasn't going to be alive after her body hit the road. All I could focus on, all I could really see, was the look of despair in her eyes as she collided with the ground. Her face and her clothes were covered in dirt and stained with blood.

"That night, I heard a noise, a noise I wouldn't wish anyone to hear, knowing it came from their loved one. It was the loudest bone-crushing crack. And I saw a mist of red surrounding Lauren's head as she landed in her final resting place on the road. She had landed head first and her skull bounced off the ground. The red mist was her blood as it left her body."

Matthew sheds tears. The lump in his throat is so big he can barely swallow. Jess holds him tight and says nothing. She pulls back, then lets him go and disappears into the kitchen for a moment, returning with a handful of gold napkins. She puts them on the edge of the table next to Matthew, who remains still and utterly broken, his head in his hands. He hasn't flinched since she left the room. She sits down next to him again.

"Do you want know something? Eve has never forgiven herself, and she's felt for years that it's *all her fault*. I know this is the reason why she gets angry: the poor child carries nothing but guilt. She's had counselling and I know she doesn't want to live. For years I haven't wanted to live either. I would've ended it all, but I know Eve would do the same, and then what? Lauren sacrificed her life so that our daughter could continue to have one – what sort of respect for her ultimate sacrifice is that? I live for Lauren's bravery, I live for Eve, because I know that's what Lauren would want."

There is a brief silence. Matthew's eyes are now red raw and almost closed from crying so many tears. His head is throbbing after revisiting the pained memories and reliving this emotionally traumatic part of his life. Matthew decides to break the silence. "I didn't want to live for a long time – it should have been me throwing myself into the road for our daughter. I had to watch the only woman I've ever loved thrown into the sky like a toy – and come back down looking full of fear.

"It didn't end there: Eve and I saw Lauren lie completely motionless in the road. Her eyes were wide open, but I could tell that Lauren's soul was no longer present – her skull was caved in on one side. She was lying in a puddle of her own blood. Not only was the ground coated – Lauren's clothes were also dripping with the blood that just wouldn't stop gushing from her head. The horrific image of blood surrounding her body is the image that stays with me day and night. That image has embedded itself deep in my memory. It lives at the forefront of my mind, appearing whenever it desires. As an adult, seeing such a horrific scene has impacted me massively, and has unlocked dark sections in my brain that I never knew existed. I can't help but wonder what impact it had on my daughter.

"Eve's such a vulnerable young lady and at that time she was practically a child. When she was little she would always stroke her mum's face. While Lauren lay there on the ground, Eve ran to her mum. Distraught, she cradled her and stroked her face. This image kills me. It hurts my heart to see my baby girl covered in her mum's blood, just holding her and screaming out, suffering. My poor Eve is forced to live the rest of her life motherless at the start of her innocent journey and yet it is fate that has dealt her this hand. Why? Her poor mind, without any warning, was left wide open to this horrific event, and now my once innocent, life-loving, adrenaline junkie, smiling Evelyn Jade is riddled with aggression and bitterness. I can't blame her for this; I was the same for a long time. The only reason I didn't continue on that path is because of my daughter. I want Eve to rebuild and gain strength from me. I live in hope that one day she will become strong again."

"Matthew, I'm speechless. How horrific for you both. As a fellow believer in fate, I'm sure life has its reasons for you both and, well, I'm here now, you are not completely alone just yet."

With these words, Jess's eyes suddenly spark and take on an overcast shadow of grey. Grabbing Matthew by the chin, she locks eyes with him and says four simple words: "I will empower her."

Embracing Jess's words, Matthew is ready to get off the subject.

"Thank you. I understand everything happens for a reason – this soul-crushing tragedy has been aligned for a purpose, yet I feel we are still waiting to discover what the true intention of it is. The worst thing is we have so many unanswered questions. Questions we will never receive closure on. I mean – why did we have to witness and go through the hardest thing anyone with a conscious mind could possibly experience, why us?" Pausing for a moment, as though he's waiting for someone to shout the answer, Matthew looks to Jess. "Fortunately, Eve and I managed to regain some form of normality. But do you want to know what the worst part of this disturbing process is?"

"Only if you want to tell me."

"What happened to Lauren was not an accident! I don't care what the police say, I believe it was done with intent, and one day, I will prove it. Neither Eve nor I have ever received closure for what happened to Lauren. It was a hit and run – the cruel coward behind the wheel didn't bother to stop. This devastating experience has never been closed. We have never received justice – and still, to this day, we have no idea who killed our beloved Lauren." Suddenly the front door bangs.

CHAPTER SIX

Ring a' Ring o' Roses

Matthew jumps. "Eve…"

He grabs a napkin from the pile next to him and quickly wipes his eyes. He gets up and as he makes his way towards the front door he's relieved to see his daughter. She's crouched down and taking off her shoes, looking deflated, fatigued and full of sadness.

Without hesitation, he heads towards Eve, and as she stands, he begins hugging her tighter than ever. They both embrace the moment. Matthew places her head on his chest, his arms wrapped tightly around her, holding Eve in a desperate attempt to make her feel safe. Holding back his tears and struggling to remain resilient to the emotions, he gently kisses her on the head and quietly says, "I love you, Evelyn Jade Honey."

Breaking down, Eve begins uncontrollably crying. "I love you more, Dad – I'm so sorry."

Matthew releases Eve's head from his arms and places both his hands on her shoulders. "Are you okay? Kidda, where on earth have you been? Look at you, you're shivering cold. Oh, Evelyn Jade Honey."

As Matthew says these words, tears form in his eyes. Making eye contact with Eve, he sees the truth: there's no getting away from the reality that stands before him. His daughter, his Evelyn Jade, this precious girl his wife gave her life to save, is standing right before him with a true expression of lifelessness. Her eyes radiate sorrow, discomfort and hurt; Matthew is devastated. What would Lauren say, looking down at her daughter in this state? Immediately he feels an immense sense of guilt. He has caused this. He has caused his daughter to endure a traumatic event by inviting a woman back to the house, when she clearly wasn't ready. Matthew hangs his head in shame. He's emotionally deflated as tears gently fall down his face. Looking at her dad with her swollen eyes, Eve places her forehead on to his. As she too looks down, she quietly responds, "I'm home now – you don't need to worry."

Hearing her voice, Matthew is filled with relief. Yes, she is home, yes, she is safe and yes, he never wants to let her go again. Matthew looks deeply at his daughter again and as he holds her tight once more, he says, "Can I get you anything?"

"No, thanks, I just wanna go to bed – my head hurts, I'm tired and cold," she replies.

Grabbing her backpack from off the floor, she makes her way up the stairs without acknowledging Jess, who is still standing in the dining room doorway. Matthew watches as his beautiful daughter makes her way up the stairs. As she goes out of sight, Matthew hangs his head and releases a deep sigh of relief. He feels a presence at the side of him; he was unaware that Jess was observing. He didn't know she was standing in the doorway the whole time. Looking flirtatious and playing with the locket around her neck, Jess seems unfazed by the height of the intense emotions within the room. Suffering with exhaustion, Matthew makes his way over to Jess.

"I'm sorry – maybe it's too soon…"

Before Matthew can say another word, Jess stops him in his tracks. She grabs his chin and kisses him, running her fingers through his hair. Almost instantly, his body surrenders to her. Guiding his hands slowly, she moves them around her waist and then up to her face. She places her forehead on to his and whispers directly into his ear, "I will relieve you both."

With his eyes shut, Matthew is breathing heavily. What is happening to his mind, his heartrate, his emotions? He's not in control of any of them. "Jess – please, will you stay the night?" he says in an almost robotic tone.

Matthew opens his eyes and looks at Jess. She says nothing and slowly guides him up the spiral black metal staircase. Without breaking eye contact, Jess stops midway. In her red dress, with her empowering energy, she looks proud, confident and in control on the higher step. She resembles a strong ruler. Her eyes remain overcast, a dark grey mist circulating inside them. On the step below, Matthew gazes up at her. He looks withdrawn and lost, like a beggar. Leaning down ever so slightly, she holds his chin in her hands. As she breathes him in her eyes take on a deceitful look and the grey mist becomes the deepest thick shade of black. The colour is so deep, her eyes almost form a mirror, and Matthew's innocent facial expression is reflected back.

With every second that passes, as this powerful unbreakable connection remains, Matthew is surrendering a molecule of his soul to her. Jess places her soft lips onto his. She kisses him gently – and any tiny seed of doubt that Matthew may have had earlier regarding this woman has now vanished.

Jess continues using the power she has. She leans to his ear once more and says, "Take me to your room."

Her breath is ice-cold, sending shivers along the nerves in his eardrum. Matthew is completely powerless and trapped in the moment. Without questioning her command he begins to guide her up the staircase. They enter his bedroom. Ordinarily filled with light and life, this now large space seems controlled by an evil unwanted entity. The four-poster bed looks sinister, and there is a dark vibration present so strong that it could make a soul abandon its physical form. Seeming satisfied, Jess shuts the huge mahogany door behind her. Placing her head on the varnish stained doorframe, she stays in this position for a second or two. With a sudden sharp twitch, Jess turns her head and faces Matthew, who is standing in his room looking lost and unsure of what to do next, his expression blank and almost angelic. This is the innocent look that a child gives his parent when he's been told off and will do anything for their forgiveness.

"Shut the curtains!" she commands.

Her eyes are now blacker than the midnight sky outside. Matthew, without any fight or query, makes his way round the four-poster bed. He approaches the window and reaches for the expensive, thick, floor-length golden curtains. The room is silent. He pulls the curtains together and his head drops as he sheds a tear, lonesome, long and lost.

"Jess…" He gets no response. Continuing, he says, "Jess – this isn't funny!"

"Do you like games, Matthew?"

"No."

Continuing her teasing ways regardless, Jess says, "That's a shame… I love playing games."

Appearing behind him, she begins to whisper directly in his ear, "Come on, Mr Honey, play with me."

He shudders.

"Do you know why I am in your life, Matthew, do you know your fate?"

Very blankly he replies, "No…"

With nothing but darkness present, Jess peers over his shoulder. She then leans into his ear and licks it. Matthew's face remains blank. A conceited grin begins to spread across her expression, as she teasingly says, "Good."

Quickly turning Matthew to face her, she makes eye contact with him and firmly feeds Matthew instructions. "Sit on the bed. We're going to play a little game, you and I…"

Unable to break eye contact or question this order, Matthew walks backwards. As he reaches the bed he's totally unable to bend his knees or control his movements. The calves on his legs hit the solid wood of the bedframe. His features stay motionless. He holds no expression on his face; his heart begins beating faster with every second that passes. His eyes fill with water. He can't blink, and so the tears fall unhindered and sink into the slight stubble on his face. The black netted curtains that hang from the dark wooden frame of the four-poster bed begin to close one by one, without assistance. The dark mysterious-looking curtains surround Matthew and Jess. Suddenly, an unwelcome force guides him back and with one final powerful gust of energy he's pushed and lies back on the bed.

Eve is fast asleep in her bed, wearing one of her mum's old nighties. She's resting peacefully, blissfully unaware of the events which are taking place in the room down the hall. Her bedroom, which is normally bright, airy and full of life, suddenly becomes the complete opposite. A dark, stagnant and gloomy energy begins to surface. Lurking shadows appear in each corner. The white netting behind the rose-gold floor-length curtains begins to blow forward ever so slightly.

The clothes Eve had on today are sprawled out in an untidy manner over the white wooden chair by her desk, which holds all her coursework. Sat on top of all the papers is one of her most sacred possessions: her diary. This isn't one of the leather-backed, scrawling notebooks that she uses to release her frustration, this is her actual personal diary! A huge metal golden buckle rests on top of its thick spine. Ordinarily this is locked, securing the pages that contain all her secrets. The deep red leather-backed book holds all her inner thoughts and true emotions. Her dad never enters her room and so Eve leaves the personal book around freely. Her backpack, its contents removed and its zip open slightly, looks deflated. It's placed on the floor next to the bed. The picture of her and her mum is proudly positioned on the solid-white wooden bedside cabinet, and this is the first thing she sees every morning.

Gregg, the scruffy bow-tied teddy-bear, is on the pillow next to her head. She fell asleep with him resting on her face. Eve often does this when she's had an emotionally challenging day. Gregg still has the sweet scent of her mum's favourite Chanel perfume on his fur, even after all these years. The teddy looks as though he's watching over her whilst she's sleeping peacefully.

Suddenly, out of nowhere, a huge gust of wind flows through the room, causing Eve to shudder in her sleep. Its presence becomes so forceful the hairs on her body stand to attention as she pulls the bedsheets up to her chin. She's still dreaming. Within a matter of seconds, the powerful gust of energy travels round the room and forces Eve's diary open. The leather-backed book stands no chance as the wind ruffles through the pages.

Eve's expression changes slightly. A look of concern, a look of fear, a look of neglect and despair, begins to surface on her face. It's as though she's making a progressive transition from dreaming sweet, pleasant dreams to soul-crushing, obnoxious, terrifying nightmares. As she turns, her face begins to sink into the pillow and she sobs ever so slightly.

The diary on her desk lies open at a double page with blue inked writing neatly scrawled all over it. The pages read the following:

It's three years since you left me, three years since you were taken away from me. Today I met someone and the only person I wanted to tell was you.

I met him on the bus and for just a brief second, I forgot all about you not being here any more! A brief second passed and I thought... Shit, what's mum going to think about me speaking to him?

He's a lot older than me and yes, he made butterflies tickle in my tummy so much that I forgot all about you being <u>DEAD</u>!

Yes, dead! You're DEAD and I must live with this! I must live with the fact that you're no longer here because of <u>ME</u>!

Your own flesh and blood!

You gifted me with life and yet I took yours from you!

Then it hits me! Eve, you don't have a mum and when this guy finds out why, he will want nothing to do with you!

You're broken and cursed, Evelyn Jade Honey.

Why should you be happy...?

Why should you have a boyfriend and a life?

You killed your dad's soul mate! Your own mum!

I know I am not worthy of life and I understand that I am not worthy of death. Death would be too kind. So, what am I worthy of? What is my purpose? Why am I still here?

A big group of girls at school call me a murderer every time they see me. I've been sat on the toilet before now and they've followed me in,

reached over the cubicle and started singing 'Eve's a murderer.' I hang my
head in shame and I don't go to the toilet at school anymore.

Why didn't I look, mum, why did I just walk out? I can't cope
anymore. What is it, why am I here to be punished in life and not worthy
of being set free with death?

There are stains on the page where her tears have fallen,
smudging the blue ink.

A faint whisper sounds through the room: "You're here for me.
I have your purpose."

Eve's dream has changed. She was dreaming sweet innocent
dreams, with bright colours, rainbows and happiness, as she bounced
through the fields holding tightly on to her mum's hand. They were
skipping, laughing and playfully rolling on the grass. Well, not
anymore. Now she's lost her mum and has ventured into the darkest
forest. No one is there, not a soul is in sight. She hears the sound of
twigs and branches snapping all around her. Her senses are enhanced
by the inner fear she feels and she is trapped in this nightmare. Eve
shouts, "Mum?"

No response.

"Who's there…?"

Again, there is no reply, and Eve can't help but realise she's
trapped. Everywhere she turns, it's the same. The trees are the same.
The brown soil beneath her feet is the same. The sky is black, without
a star in sight; it's as though the universe has disappeared. The energy
radiating through her body is like a surge of electricity and is making
her heart race even faster. Feeling a strong aura, as though *she's not*
alone, and something evil is in her presence, Eve stops and remains
extremely still. With only her chest moving as she breathes in deep,
Eve looks up to the midnight sky. Feeling more vulnerable than ever,
she shouts, "Help!"

Eve falls to the floor. Her hands are cupped, holding her heavy
head as her sobbing gets louder. In the emptiness of the forest, Eve's
cries echo through the identical haunted looking trees and circulates
in the air. The ambiance is still. There isn't a mist or any living thing

to be seen. The eerie, dark trees are motionless. Eve reluctantly opens her eyes and glances through the gaps in her fingers; she sees nothing but darkness surrounding her. Any animal present would easily be able to sniff her out by the amount of fear she's oozing. She can hear her own heart beating and the sound of her breath leaving her body. Her thoughts become loud. They are thoughts of sheer panic as her mind goes into overdrive.

Accepting her fate, Eve curls herself up on the cold earthy floor surrounded by dirt and twigs. Suddenly, she picks up a vibration. Lifting her head slightly, she holds her breath. Again, she hears and feels the same vibration. Desperate to work out what it is, Eve is deep in concentration. The sound is faint; struggling, she manages to hear the tone. It's a female's voice. The sound is distant and almost sounds like singing. With her senses the strongest they've been, this enchanting voice is becoming established with every millisecond, and is now getting closer. She closes her eyes. With her sight gone, Eve's hearing is now stronger. She's almost certain it's a female voice. She appears to be singing a familiar song or nursey rhyme. Eve speaks out: "Mum?"

No response. She focuses all her sense of hearing on the sound. Closing her eyes tighter than ever, Eve is desperate to make out what the familiar song is. Suddenly, she hears the words – the mysterious enchanting voice is singing "Ring a' Ring o' Roses", but the words aren't quite right. Eve wonders if it is, in fact, her mum. Sitting up, covered in dirt and autumnal leaves, she frantically looks around her. She's desperate to see her mum again, even if it is in a dark haunted forest in the middle of nowhere. At the top of her voice Eve shouts, "Mum!"

She suddenly hears the words of the nursery rhyme echoing around the forest. The voice doesn't sound at all familiar. Lauren loved to sing this rhyme to Eve when she was a small baby girl, and yet the tone seems quite depressing, daunting and soulless. Still holding hope in her heart that it is her mum, again Eve speaks: "Mum, please, if it's you, just answer me. I'm scared."

Instantly she hears, "Ring a' Ring o' Roses – your soul is mine. Ring a' Ring o' Roses – you've been chosen for the dark side."

As these final words travel through her ears into her mind, Eve jumps up off the ground. The nightie she's wearing gets caught round her ankles and she stumbles slightly. Righting herself, Eve runs as fast as she can through the forest, making no attempt whatsoever to watch where she's going, as multiple twigs snap under her feet. With the adrenaline rushing around her body stronger than ever, Eve no longer feels pain.

Waving her arms frantically in front of her, she desperately attempts to whack the branches out of the way. Her arms and face are continually scratched. It's as though the trees and bushes are alive, reaching out to restrain her. One of the branches scratches her left arm so deeply that blood flows out. Becoming out of breath, but having no desire to stop, Eve hears loud female laughter surrounding her. No matter how far she runs, it's as though the voice is travelling in the air – embedding its existence into her pores and resonating deep within her mind. The voice is stalking and taunting her. Again, Eve clearly hears the words of the daunting nursery rhyme being repeated, over and over and over.

Exhausted, she finally stops. With no more fight left in her, she helplessly surrenders and falls to the ground, sobbing. Her lungs feel raw. Sore, and with nowhere left to go, she lies on top of the dirt, twigs and leaves. Reluctantly, Eve sits up and turns to face the darkness. The trees she's just frantically ran through appear haunting.

Eve's eyes protrude out of their sockets. Appearing from out of the dark eerie mist is a female silhouette. She's elegantly flowing and making her way towards her. Eve instantly makes a connection with this female form. Enticed by her grace and presence, Eve is unable to break free. Embracing every individual word of the possessive nursey rhyme, Eve is captivated.

"Ring a' Ring o' Roses – your soul is mine. Ring a' Ring o' Roses – you've been chosen for the dark side."

Physically frozen, Eve's mind continues to race. She's traumatised by the horrific image.

"Why are you following me… Mum… Please, is that you?"

There is no answer. The only words Eve can hear are the continually repeated nursery rhyme sung in the same dulcet tone.

Submissively surrendering herself on the cold earthy ground, Eve screams out louder than ever: "Argh..."

She covers her ears with her hands and folds herself into the foetal position, rocking back and forth. Her face, her energy and her body are expressing pain, agony and desperation. With tears gushing and exhaustion in her tone, making her sound hoarse, Eve shouts one final time, "Mum – please stop... I'm sorry."

With a sudden gasp of air, Eve shoots up from her pillow. She's soaking wet from head to toe with sweat. Immediately, she touches her head and chest to ensure she's in one piece. Relieved and wanting to run to her dad, Eve jumps off the bed and attempts to head towards the bedroom door. But as soon as both her feet hit the cold dark wooden floor, she loses the use of her legs and falls to the ground. Hysterical, she screams out, "Help!"

Almost straightaway, she hears someone heading towards her room. Still traumatised and in distress, Eve begins to drag her limp, heavy body across the floor and heads towards the desk to hide under it. A gust of wind blows through the bedroom again, rippling the curtains. Suddenly, the female silhouette from her nightmare appears in her room. Only this time, Eve can see her clearly. Her jet-black hair hangs heavy and straight, and travels past her thighs. It's separated equally on either side of her face. The hair is soaked with a thick black substance. The sinister-looking liquid travels down each strand and lands on the floor where she stands. Her eyes stand out through the gap in her hair. They're as red as human blood. Not a speck of white can be seen. An overwhelming surge of anxiety travels through Eve and begins taking over. She's so shocked she can't even cry. She sits, silent in disbelief at the image her eyes are projecting into her mind.

Slowly, the female form begins making her way across the room to Eve. With every step she takes, the black substance drips from her. Eve's eyes transform and become dark as she gazes at this seemingly evil entity. Completely engrossed and fixated on her presence, Eve remains in a solid trance.

"Ring a' Ring o' Roses – your soul is mine. Ring a' Ring o' Roses – you've been chosen for the dark side."

In these spilt seconds, Eve embraces the words being fed to her. The rhythm and vibration of this possessive rhyme enter her mind. It's becoming part of her blood flow and embedding deep within her DNA. It travels through Eve's internal organs as it makes its way towards Eve's eyes, taking over her sight. Her nerves tingle as her eyes begin to change. It's as though someone is repeatedly stabbing tiny needles into her eyeballs. This sadistic possession is taking over her body and is claiming her soul – her innocent soul, which is now accepting its fate.

A huge *bang* sounds in the background. Eve breaks contact with the shadowy woman and screams even louder than before. This time, she doesn't stop.

Suddenly, the dark woman appears right in front of Eve's face. This time, Eve sees the truth. She sees her full expression. The evil entity's skin is entirely grey. She's covered with black cracks, which are spread all over her physical form. These deep embedded rips drip with the same sinister, thick, black bloody substance that fills her hair. The black oozes from around her mouth and from the centre of her grey soulless lips. Placing her grey forefinger, which has deep marks upon it, to Eve's mouth, she signs, "Shh...."

The black substance gushes out of her mouth and continues its descent down her chin, landing on the floor. Her temperature is ice-cold. Her finger stays on Eve's mouth, the texture skin-crawling. It's hard and rough. Eve's nostrils are awakened by a pungent stench that leaves a metallic bloody taste in her mouth. The black substance begins to make its unwanted way to the back of her throat, growing at a rapid rate. Eve is powerless to remove it from her internal body. It's taking over. Her mouth is wide open, but no sound is coming out.

Matthew kicks violently at Eve's bedroom door, but the sturdy fixture doesn't yield. The solid golden doorknob rattles as he desperately tries to get to his daughter. He's repeatedly shouting, "Eve... Unlock the door, Eve..."

The doorknob turns one final time and the door opens. Matthew stumbles into the room wearing nothing but his green and white checked pyjama bottoms and a white-gold chain with a solid silver cross around his neck. As he gains control of his balance, Matthew looks around the dark and mysteriously eerie room, completely alone.

"Eve…"

In a state of panic, his breathing becomes heavy as his fear heightens. He looks at the bed. It's messy, empty and no one can be seen. He hears a knock come from behind him that sounds like the tapping of bone. Matthew's breathing rate increases rapidly. The room has developed a sub-zero temperature and he sees his breath leaving his body. The hairs on his skin stand to attention. With every deep breath he takes, the sub-zero atmosphere in the room travels around him. He notices a familiar, nauseating stench that develops into an equally disturbing taste at the back of his throat. He feels unwell. The fear of the unknown has taken over his mind.

"Eve… Is that you…?"

Jess suddenly rushes into the room behind him, covering her naked body with Matthew's black silk dressing gown. "Matthew, what's going on?"

He doesn't answer. His eyes are now the only parts of his body that are moving. Suddenly, his ears twitch as he hears a shuffling sound and feels a vibration coming from under the desk. He makes his way towards the sound and without so much of a second thought, he reaches out and pulls back the chair. He drags it so hard that the chair and all the clothes on top of it fly across the room. Kneeling, he moves towards the gap under the desk. As he bends and looks to the floor, he notices tiny spots of black liquid leading like a trail underneath the desk. More anxious than ever, Matthew's now wondering not who, but what, is actually hiding under the desk. His body shaking, he suddenly feels an immense sense of relief.

"Eve… There you are."

Putting out his arms, he reaches under the desk to hold his frail, timid-looking daughter. Eve releases an horrific ear-piercing scream.

"Ahh!"

Matthew leaps back in shock and Eve jumps, banging her head on the wooden desk top.

In desperation, Matthew shouts, "Eve, it's me. Dad."

Peering under the desk from a safe distance, he's horrified by what he sees. Eve's eyes are jet-black – no white can be seen. She's laughing insanely at nothing. Her skin tone is changing with every second that passes. She's turning a sinister shade of grey. Focusing her attention towards her dad, Eve's head begins to move closer to him. The energy oozing from her feels strongly psychotic. Matthew once again leaps back, except this time, he leaps so high he practically throws himself and his spine hits against the wooden frame of Eve's bed. Full of shock at what he's witnessing, Matthew turns to Jess, who is stood in the doorway. She has her hand on her chest and is holding the locket round her neck. Her expression seems unnatural for the current situation. She appears calm.

Eve slowly appears from under the desk, looking directly towards her dad who is motionless. Matthew's face is still and radiates fear. His slightly hairy chest expands with every deep breath he takes. He watches as Eve reaches out with her right arm and places each of her fingertips onto the floor, one by one. Her thumb is the last to land. Her hand now resembles the long legs of a spider, and Eve begins to drag her heavy body from under the desk. As the air hits her physical form, Eve's skin tone continues to darken.

Watching this transformation take place, Matthew remains still. "Please, Lord – save our souls… Please, Lord, I beg you, save our souls…" he whispers.

Eve reaches out with her left arm in the same manner, and this time her head follows. She looks down at the blood leaving her body, dripping from a deep cut on her arm. It appears red as it seeps through the rip in her skin, but then changes to black. Eve suddenly stops. Slowly she turns to face Jess. Their eyes lock and the pair connect. Eve's skin changes. As she stretches out her face, deep cracks begin to form, like gaping holes in her body. Matthew looks again to Jess, who seems unnaturally content. She slowly steps backwards out of the room, gently placing one foot behind the other, being careful not to break eye contact with Eve. Jess's expression oozes pride.

With Jess out of the room, Eve turns her attention back towards her dad and her face turns venomous. She drags her heavy, limp body towards him as black blood drips from her mouth and smears across the floor. *"Darmi la tua anima e non ucciderò, darmi la tua anima,"* she repeats in a deep tone.

Matthew is panicked. He's unable to process the words she's saying as she moves closer to him. His head begins to spin. He's petrified, his body stuck in a mysterious trance. He has an item in his hand, which he's holding onto tightly. The white-gold chain hangs from the creases of his hand. Slowly he opens his fingers and reveals the solid silver cross. There are imprints from the edges of the cross embedded in the palm of his hand. Eve's eyes dart to the shimmering cross. She immediately stops, her facial expression is confused. Suddenly a gust of wind blows and the bedroom door *slams* shut, locking Jess on the other side. Looking down to the floor, Eve hears these words circulating inside her mind: "Your soul is mine!"

She lifts her head and her eyes are filled with pure hatred along with a dark evil energy. She raises her leg in an acrobatic manner, her toes pointing perfectly to the ground. Her expression grows darker and darker. Her eyes are completely black; not a shade of white is present. They are like bottomless holes in her face. Dragging her body, Eve now moves faster and faster towards her dad, leaving smears of thick black blood on the floor behind her. Matthew remains frozen, tears of faith falling rapidly down his motionless face. He's now gripping the cross so tightly that it cuts through his skin. Deep red blood begins dripping from the cross, falling from the creases in his hand to the floor.

As Eve reaches her dad he holds the cross out and she instantly collapses. Her arms fall, and her legs go flat. Her body lands in a heap. Eve begins convulsing on the ground. A black substance foams from her mouth and her eyes are cloudy.

Slowly, her eyes return to their normal colour. Her face twitches. It's as though an evil entity is leaving her physical form and letting go of her soul. With every second that passes, her expression becomes less demonic and her skin is returning to her normal tone.

The deep rips in Eve's flesh begin healing on their own. The black blood dripping from each limb is absorbed back into her skin. The black foam travels down her chin and also begins to disappear. Eve now lies motionless. Feeling his heart beating as his own daughter is extremely close to him, Matthew is filled with terror.

Not knowing what to do next, he hears a creek and turns to the door. It's beginning to open. Jess, who was standing in the hallway, peers into the room from a distance. Once again, she's proudly holding the locket around her neck. Matthew doesn't speak. His breathing has become so heavy and erratic he looks as though, at any given moment, he's going to pass out. Attempting to create some distance between him and Eve, as a precaution, he pushes his limp, stiff body onto her bed. Eve lies lifeless on the floor; she is motionless. Just like her mum when she died, it looks as though her soul has left her physical form. Matthew whispers, "Eve…"

Suddenly, he feels an overwhelming surge of breathlessness as his head begins spinning round. It's as though he has been spiked with drugs. His sight goes blurry, his hearing fades and his head becomes heavy. The room is spinning at such a rapid rate he feels as though he's about to throw up. He becomes extremely light-headed. The last thing he sees is an outline of Jess heading towards him. She's looking somewhat pleased with herself. Hearing his own voice one final time, he says, "Eve…" Slowly, this begins to echo inside his mind.

He's out!

CHAPTER SEVEN

The Games Begin!

Matthew hesitantly opens his eyes and sees only darkness surrounding him. Jet-black to the left and jet-black to the right; no fixtures, no fittings, *nothing*. An eerie energy begins travelling through his pores, into his veins, and resonates within his mind. It's telling him *he's not alone*.

Matthew is desperate to discover where he is. Riddled with anxiety, which grows with every second of the unknown that passes, he reaches out his hands and places them directly in front of his body. He slowly moves his arms around and it's as if they are floating. He attempts to feel for anything. But still he sees, and feels, nothing.

As his sight adjusts he places his hands a few inches away from his face, waving them slowly. He can see his tiny freckles, hairs and scruffy bitten nails. He turns them over and looks into his palms. He's shocked at what he sees. In his right palm there is dark red, thick blood, along with four deep imprints. Blood drips from each cut and collects together to form a cross. His stomach turns. No longer able to hold it, he vomits next to where he stands. It evaporates almost instantly. A sickening acid taste remains at the back of his throat. Matthew feels ill and scared. He spits in an attempt to remove the taste from his mouth. Before he vomits once more, he bravely shouts, "Hello, can anyone hear me? Eve?"

No response. His eyes become overcast and heavy. His temples start to throb and the fear of the unknown is getting too much for him to bear. Feeling more vulnerable than ever, Matthew looks dead ahead; still, he sees nothing but darkness. The only sound is of his breath as it leaves his body. He tries bravely to suppress the fear he feels. Finding his inner courage, he shouts, "Hello, can anyone hear me?"

He doesn't know whether to feel relieved by the deadly silence or even more fearful as the evil presence surrounding him appears to be getting stronger. Not knowing who, or what, owns this energy, but feeling as though it isn't the blessing from the Lord Christ himself, Matthew breathes in and closes his eyes. His legs become weak. Desperately trying to dig deep and locate every inch of his inner strength so he doesn't collapse, Matthew looks down at his appearance. He's still wearing the green and white checked pyjama pants and he can just make out the flesh showing at the bottom from his bare feet. Looking beyond his body, he appears to be standing on *nothing*. *No* floor. *No* ceiling. It's as though he's floating on a jet-black blanket of air, standing alone in the universe with no stars, no planets, just an abyss of nothing, as though life itself never existed.

Imprisoned by his own thoughts, Matthew absorbs the fear this evil entity is feeding his mind. Closing his eyes, he says, "Come on, Matthew, it's all in your head. You just need to wake up."

Opening his eyes, he fiercely begins shouting at the top of his voice, "What do you want from me?"

Surrendering to the darkness, he lies down, a broken man. He's completely unaware of the deception he has so cunningly been thrown into. Such a calculated and scheming trap. Unknowingly, Matthew has converted to the evil entity's desires. This once strong man is now a victim to the shackles of his own mind. He sobs gently, holding his head in his hands with his eyes still closed. Suddenly he hears a female voice echoing towards him.

"Do you like to play games, Mr Honey?"

Lifting his head from out of his hands, the only desire Matthew has *right now* is to break free and find his daughter. And so, he chooses to say nothing.

Again, he hears, "Do you like to play games, Mr Honey? Ring a' Ring o' Roses—"

"What do you want from me?" he interrupts with saliva flying uncontrollably from his mouth, irritated by the suggested games.

There is a long pause. Suddenly, he hears an echo resonating in the distance. This calms him slightly as his aggression subsides. Closing his eyes and tuning in his ears, he soon works out, it's *him*. His own voice is mockingly echoing around him. Placing his head back into his hands, he closes his eyes. No sooner has he shut off his sight, Matthew's mind begins to project a disturbing memory. He hears the screams of his innocent young Eve. He sees her face as she watches her mum collide with the ground, covered in her own blood. Distraught by this vision, he covers his ears and screams out in agony, "Eve!"

A pungent stench once again begins to take over his nostrils and explore the back of his throat. Matthew chokes on the metallic taste. Curled up, he feels as though someone has taken a blade to his organs and they're slowly ripping through each one. There is nowhere to turn and not a glimmer of hope in sight. Eventually the teasing female voice reappears.

"Don't cry, Mr Honey, your purpose is aligned – you will soon receive your fate."

With these words, the female entity releases a psychotic laugh. The insane laughter begins embedding itself inside Matthew's eardrums, and as it circulates, it implants its unwanted existence deep within his mind. Matthew screams louder and louder, in a desperate attempt to drown it out. Tears form in his eyes and fall down his face. "Let me out... Let me out... Let me out..." he screams.

Feeling exposed, weak and vulnerable, he lies on his side, his knees tucked to his chest and his hands stuck to his ears, desperately attempting to prevent the psychotic laughter from entering further into his mind. Squeezing his eyes together tightly, he feels as though he's crying thick tears of blood. And then, for the second time, his mind goes blank and there is only nothingness.

Matthew leaps forward with a sudden *gasp*. He's unexplainably in his own bed, soaking wet from head to toe, wearing nothing but his boxer shorts. He tries to call out to Eve, but he's lost his voice.

The room is empty. The perfectly painted white walls appear bright as the sun peers through the gap in the curtains. The mood in the room is calm and still.

Touching his face and wiping the sweat off his head, Matthew lies back and coughs as he struggles to clear his dry throat. He reaches for the glass of water on the bedside table and takes a sip, wondering whether he is losing his mind. Still in a daze, he begins to wonder where Eve is. He pushes his legs out from underneath the bedsheets. They suddenly feel stiff and heavy. He shuffles to the side of the four-poster bedframe, feeling as if he has almost no energy, and slowly slumps to the floor. His sight becomes blurry. Gradually he raises his head. Feeling pathetic, Matthew lies with his head on the edge of his bed. He's so tired. The entrapment begins to replay in his mind; he hears the psychotic laughter of the woman and her teasing words as they play on repeat in his head, like a scratched disk.

Another undesired memory surfaces. He sees Lauren's soulless face and cracked skull flash in his mind. Closing his eyes tight, he shakes his head in a desperate attempt to remove this image from his vision. As soon as he opens his eyes once more, Matthew's mind projects another image. It's Eve. She's curled up on the ground next to her dead mum, uncontrollably crying. With salvia running down her chin and fluid gushing from her nose, she's screaming, "Mum, come back to me, I'm sorry. Mum, please, don't go. Somebody do something. Dad, *save* her."

Reliving this horrific moment, suddenly he sees himself, and he's not helping or doing anything to save his wife; he's frozen on the ground next to her battered body and isn't moving. He closes his eyes again to remove the image. Matthew's determined this time he isn't going to surrender and become frozen with fear. Pushing himself up using all the upper body strength he can, slowly he rises off the ground. Now standing on his feet, he manages to steadily take one step at a time as he gradually makes his way across to the bedroom door.

Exhausted and fragile, finally he reaches the wooden doorframe. Instantly, he loses his balance and collapses whilst still holding onto the golden doorknob. Mentally drained, he quietly begins to sob as he presses his head against the wall. He hears voices clearly in his mind. Female voices. But the tone isn't haunting, sad or full of sorrow, it's laughter; it's happy, joyous laughter.

It's *Eve*. He can hear her. Hearing her voice is like an injection of life administered directly into his veins. Dragging himself up, he attempts to stand once again and this time he triumphs. Gathering enough strength, he reaches out and successfully opens the bedroom door. Feeling a sharp pain shoot up his right arm, Matthew lets go of the golden doorknob and looks into the palm of his hand. He sees the four deep cuts which are spread out and shaped like a cross.

Matthew glances down to his chest. The white chain along with the cross is *gone*. All that remains in its place are tiny spots of what he believes is his own blood mixed with a small amount of his chest hair. He hasn't taken the chain off since the day Lauren gave it to him almost four years ago, on their final Valentine's day together.

Hoping the chain came off in bed and is in his bedsheets, Matthew is now standing in the hallway. The mood is the complete opposite of the last time he stood in this very same spot. It's now bright, airy and filled with life. The pure white painted walls are complimented beautifully by the exquisite bright pieces of art hanging perfectly parallel on the walls.

Suddenly he hears Eve. She's laughing away downstairs. Still unsteady on his feet, he slowly places one foot in front of the other. Feeling slightly weaker than before, Matthew approaches the top of the spiral staircase.

Standing like a statue, looking to the task in front of him, he sees each step beginning to stretch out. His breathing rate changes, becoming out of sync with his body. He has an overwhelming sense of nausea and becomes light-headed as the ground beneath him spins. Daunted by the challenge the staircase presents him with, he suddenly hears Eve's voice getting closer. His heart begins to warm and his eyes form tears of relief as he sees her. She has appeared from the kitchen looking cheery, well rested and full of life. Satisfied now that he has seen his daughter, and thankfully she's okay, Matthew collapses on the top step. Grabbing the metal rail as he falls, he places his head on the cold, metal bars.

"It was just a dream," he says quietly to himself.

Relief sinks in as he hears Eve shout out to someone, "My God, Dad. Help, quickly, he's collapsed…"

As he opens his eyes slightly, daylight beams through the glass surrounding the front door, and glows like a torch into his eyes. Squinting and in somewhat of a daze, he can just make out Eve's worried and concerned face. With his vocal chords still refusing to resume to their normal tone, he sounds as though he's losing his life.

"Eve, there you are. Please, I've been looking for you."

Again, he hears Eve speaking to someone in a panic. But he doesn't know who it is.

"Help me, please. I think we should take him to the hospital. Dad. Can you hear me?"

Matthew hears a familiar voice in the distance.

"Matthew…"

Peering through the tiny slits in his eyes, he sees a woman walking up the staircase and heading towards him with a sliver shimmer. He notices a beautiful star-like glisten around the woman's neck. Almost instantly, his expression becomes happy. "Lauren," he says hoarsely, reaching out his arms. "Lauren – it's really you. You came back."

"What's happening…?" Eve says, sounding panicked.

The woman he believes is Lauren kneels at the side of him on the step. Still smiling, Matthew turns to face her. The daylight isn't as bright anymore and as he opens his eyes fully, he sees the truth. It's *not* Lauren, it's *not* his soul mate, it's a very concerned-looking Jess, with a locket around her neck glistening away, and next to her kneels a scared and concerned-looking Eve. Turning to Jess, confused, Matthew says, "I don't understand, what's going on?" Looking to his daughter he continues, "Eve…"

But, before Eve has time to answer, Jess says, "It's okay, Matthew, don't worry, you just had a bit of a strange turn last night. I think it was a bad dream. You were randomly shouting in your sleep and dripping with sweat."

"But I don't understand, Eve, you... weren't you... your skin turned grey, and you were in trouble. Eve, your eyes. They were black, and you had black blood down your face."

Eve stops her dad. "Dad, honestly, I'm fine. Like Jess said, it was a bad dream – nothing to worry about with me." Holding her dad's hand, she continues, "It's you I'm worried about."

Confused, he's in a slight panic as both Jess and Eve are practically confirming that he's, in fact, losing his mind. Matthew turns to Jess in the hope of receiving some form of reassurance.

"Jess, you were there, you were just as petrified as I was."

Immediately, Jess turns to face Eve. She nods her head and Eve, again, speaks up. "Dad – seriously, it was just a nightmare. I'm fine, you're fine, Jess is fine—"

Matthew interrupts. "Hang about... When did you two become best friends?"

Still kneeling on the staircase, Eve, who was staring at Jess, turns back to look at her dad. She stands and reaches out to lift him from off the step.

"Dad, come on, don't worry about that, we're fine. You need to concentrate on getting better. Now, let's take you back to bed. Time to rest."

Helping her dad to stand, Eve carries him up the stairs.

Reaching his room, she guides her dad and places him on his bed. Positioning herself at his bedside, she gently begins to stroke his face.

"Dad, I love you. Please rest and promise me you'll stay in bed."

"Okay, darling, I promise."

Matthew's just as concerned for his own wellbeing. He's confused, exhausted and simply desires nothing more than to feel himself again. Slowly surrendering to the bed, he can feel himself about to drift off.

"Will you be okay?"

Stroking back her dad's hair, Eve whispers, "Of course I will. Jess is all right, and, well, to be honest, you really gave her a fright last night. She was so scared. And, well, between the pair of us, Dad, I'm kind of surprised she's still here."

Now more confused than ever, he begins to question himself. Was it really just a nightmare? It felt so real. Looking down, he can still see the cuts on his hand. Eve holds him tight. As she lets go, she cups his face and says one final word, "Sleep."

Sinking into the mattress, the soft Egyptian cotton sheets embracing his skin, Matthew's eyelids begin to close as all his energy leaves his body. With one final glance, he sees Eve leaving the room and as she closes the door behind her, he notices a bandage on her left arm. But it's too late. He whispers, "Eve." *He's out…*

Once again, Matthew is falling back into the darkness with his eyes firmly closed. No sooner has he escaped the traumatic nightmare than he's *back*. Locked within his own mind. Falling deeper and deeper into the abyss of his inner soul, he becomes paralysed with fear. He's falling into the jet-black, no longer in control of the movements of his body. Like a helpless individual who drowns at the hands of the vicious parts of the sea, Matthew's drowning at the hands of his soul. It's as though his spinal cord has been removed from his skeleton. Motionless, deflated, collapsing, Matthew surrenders himself. Within a few short seconds of his helpless submission, a powerful force awakens around him.

With one final descent, his body has sunk. He's no longer falling. He lands in a seated position. His eyes closed, Matthew feels an overwhelming surge of anxiety regarding his fate. Frozen to his surroundings and feeling suffocated, Matthew once again feels an energy surging through his veins. This powerful sinister energy field is letting him know, yet again, *he's not alone.*

His nerves slowly begin to activate, enhancing his ability to feel pain. His eyes closed, he breathes deeply. His lungs stretch and aren't even close to their maximum capacity. Suddenly, Matthew's chest becomes tight. It's as though someone's sat suppressing his ribcage as he takes each breath. The strong sensation from the movement of his chest feels extremely intense. Matthew's in agony. It feels like each individual rib is snapping and piercing its way through the layers of tissue surrounding his lungs. He's struggling to breathe.

He is in excruciating pain and at a huge disadvantage as he is unable to influence, or control, any movement of his body. The powerful presence he has surrendered himself to is leading all his senses. Suddenly, the muscles and nerves behind his eyes begin twitching. His eyelids uncontrollably flicker. Paralyzed, Matthew's aware he isn't creating this spasm. In a desperate attempt to keep his eyes closed and wanting to stay away from the reality that's present before him, Matthew tries to battle against the movement, but he's unsuccessful. His eyes pop open as if someone has ripped his eyelids apart. He's unable to fight it any longer. He can feel each wriggling blood vessel in his eyes as his pupils dilate and adjust to the light that is appearing in the distance.

As he regains his sight, Matthew realises he can control the movement of his eyes. He puts all his focus on the light that's forming in the distance. The strange single beam looks like a small star in the sky at night. Unwillingly Matthew begins to accept his fate. But before this acceptance takes over, he unexpectedly hears a voice present in his captured mind. Entirely restrained at the hands of this torturous, evil presence, he turns his attention to the voice he hears so clearly. He's quick to realise, yet again, it's his own voice. He feels no connection to the words, or the tone, whatsoever. The characteristics are almost unrecognisable. The words Matthew hears himself speaking are, "Whatever my fate, I ask you to free me – if death is in my cards, please let my soul know she's gone with no return. If life is in my cards, please let my soul live free and tell me how I can bring her back."

Remaining completely paralysed and unable to speak, Matthew questions what this could mean.

Wondering whether he's receiving some form of clue, Matthew tries to piece things together.

"Bring her back to me. Lauren's gone."

He's quiet, as though he's waiting for the answer. But with no response, Matthew's powerless. He's only just broken free from one entrapment, and he has absolutely no desire to go through the same games all over again. With his previously traumatic experience still fresh in his mind, he begins slowly to realise that his current situation is far more concerning than the last. At least then he had the ability to move freely. This time, he's completely unable to control or influence any of his movements. The only thing he can control is his eyes, which, given his current state, doesn't seem so much like an advantage to him.

The light in the distance is getting brighter. Desperate to regain possession of his body, he stares attentively at the enchanting beam, trying to work out what it is. Suddenly, he develops a new sensation within his lower body. With aches in his feet, and pain in his legs, Matthew's body unexpectedly begins to move, in a very controlled motion. But this movement is once again not in *his* control. Every rock forward is timed to perfection, and each movement back is in sync with the next. The continual sequence feels calculated his body moves back and forth. Matthew's completely incapable of stopping this. It's as if he's under a deep state of hypnosis. As the light gets closer, he can see his surroundings. He senses a strange presence at his side, which doesn't *at all* feel friendly. Petrified, Matthew breathes faster and faster.

Unaware of who, or what, is present, Matthew reluctantly plucks up his courage. Slowly he begins to focus his sight to the space at the side of his rocking body. The movement is big, and yet he can't hear a single thing. The experience is supernatural and strange; it's as though a scene is changing at a theatre production, except there is no one moving the stage props and pulling wires to change the backdrop. As he peers out of the corner of his eye, a pain shoots through his nerves. Natural daylight begins to beam towards him. Squinting his eyes in an attempt to adjust his sight to the bright vision, Matthew is stunned. He sees a window has formed. Straining to see the view out of the mysterious window, he's at a huge disadvantage, but for some unknown reason, Matthew feels a weird sense of familiarity with the structure. He recognises it but it's too far away to make out the specific details. Straining one final time, he's convinced he's seen it before. It virtually looks, and feels, as if he's seeing the window in his dayroom. The very same window he stands in front of most mornings.

He looks deeper and deeper. Matthew's eyes can't take the straining any longer and he turns his sight away. The pain becomes too unbearable. Still paralysed, he can't move his head, which makes him incapable of confirming if this is, in fact, his window. The window is only just in his peripheral vision and it almost feels like a cruel intentional trap. The light appearing in front of him becomes brighter as Matthew's body continues to rock back and forth.

Looking dead ahead, he sees a mirror has appeared. It's full-length and standing tall. Again, this object feels *familiar*... It's extremely similar to the one standing proudly with its gold frame at the bottom of the staircase at home. Matthew begins to centre his focus on the reflection in the mirror. In the reflective glass, he sees himself. He's sat in a dark wooden rocking chair, and is silently rocking back and forth, in a controlled motion.

Matthew feels an overwhelming surge of emotions: a deep internal sense of loss, depression, lifelessness and evil revenge. Caught off guard, he suffers an intense amount of uncontrollable agony. He feels his heart actually *break*!

Unable to shout out, Matthew begins to breathe rapidly. He feels each blood vessel of his heart crush. Tears begin to form in his eyes. Once again, he hears his voice. The words he speaks. "I will find her..."

No sooner has this circulated in his mind than Matthew hears and sees himself laughing insanely. In excruciating pain, and more confused than ever, Matthew questions what he's hearing.

CHAPTER EIGHT

Premonition... Maybe?

L ooking deep into the mirror, Matthew sees his body is top-heavy and slumped with his head hanging low. His jawline is resting on his chest. He looks like a patient who has been sedated. He turns his attention to the bottom of the mirror, engrossed by what he can see. Matthew is wearing a pair of black boots which are dirty and covered with grey dust. This look is not representative of his usual immaculate and smart appearance. His feet are placed perfectly parallel on the floor and are moving in synchronisation with the rocking motion. Seeing this, Matthew finally understands why he has been feeling the rocking forward and backward motion. It's surreal, as the movement of his body remains totally out of his control. Looking either side of his feet, he sees the flat, dark, wooden rocker rails on the chair; the movement of these slats of wood mirrors the slow rocking.

His gaze gradually travels up his body. He's wearing the faded ripped jeans Eve bought him as a joke one Christmas. On the tag she wrote, "Welcome to the twenty-first century, Dad." He has only worn the jeans once, and yet here he sits, looking as though he's been wearing them for the past few months. Dirty, faded black material. Matthew can see his flesh peering through the rips on his knees. He notices both his hands are crossed and resting on his lap. This instantly grabs his attention, as he never sits this way. Focusing all his energy on this spot, he becomes aware that he's securely holding on to something, but he can't quite make it out. Getting frustrated, Matthew wants nothing more than to understand why this is happening to him. With what little amount of internal strength he has to fight against this entrapment, he shouts, "Move, Matthew, please, *just move.*"

He hears his voice, but the harsh reality is it's only in his head. Looking into the mirror, Matthew sees his mouth hasn't moved, and neither has his body. Running out of options to release himself from this trap, Matthew's only hope is to piece together the puzzle of his current unfortunate state. His eyes continue to rock back and forth and Matthew feels nauseous. Determined to succeed, he looks into his lap. Matthew sees he's holding a picture frame. Once again, he feels a sense of familiarity with this item. He tries in vain to make out the image inside the frame. Being unable to move his head places him at a great disadvantage. He has no chance of seeing the image, it's *too* far away. Trying to work out a piece of the puzzle gives him internal strength. He's determined he's not giving up and brings his attention to his other hand, which grips another item tightly. Straightaway, he works out what it is.

He stares in complete shock and disbelief, his breathing getting heavier. Resting on his lap and held tightly in his hand is a black 9mm pistol, and attached to this is a protruding black silencer. As soon as he sees this, his mind starts to race.

"Please, Lord, forgive me, what have I done?"

He's now more scared than ever. Matthew's thoughts have become a mist of combined madness. He suddenly hears insane female laughter. Extremely worn out, he questions his purpose; he has never held a gun in his life. Desiring answers, but not receiving them any time soon, he begins an attempt at piecing together what he sees in the mirror.

"I've got a picture in one hand – and a lethal weapon in the other."

His eyes are starting to feel pained from all the straining. Blocking out the screaming and unbearable insanity circulating within his mind, Matthew recalls something he said. Something he now considers an important piece of the puzzle.

"I said I'd find her. Find who... who is she?"

Remaining helplessly trapped and no closer to freeing himself, Matthew's almost ready to submit and surrender to the demands of whoever or whatever is taunting his innocent soul. Looking deep into the reflection he can't help but grieve for the man he once was. The same strong Matthew Honey who now seems like a distant memory. Thinking of Eve, instantly he feels a sense of happiness, if only for a brief second; it doesn't matter. In this snapshot moment, Matthew isn't filled with discomfort and pain. He sees his best friend and an intense sense of power generates inside him, making him stronger. He must break free; he must fight for his daughter.

A voice begins echoing within the realms of the room. The words are unclear, but nonetheless, the voice is present. Ready for the next challenge, Matthew is alert. Is it Eve? With his ears finely tuned, he hears and feels himself breathing deeply, every inhale and exhale. He frantically looks around through the reflection in the mirror.

He notices a grey mist that has begun to seep around him. It begins to surround his feet, along with the rocker rails on the chair. This unnerving mist has not entered alone. Travelling with this substance is an evil and deceitful energy. He looks deeper into the mirror, but there's not a soul present. But the mysterious dark mist is getting thicker. Surrounded by a suppressive, devious energy, which appears to be binding the mist together, Matthew feels as if this is it: this is his final command of fate.

The dark energy begins to reveal its true self, becoming strong and dominant. It has full advantage over the situation as it rises in the room. It is ice-cold and, as the mist thickens, it circulates inside his boots. The sub-zero temperature gives him a sense of feeling in each of his toes; it's a tingling pin-like sensation. Thousands of tiny nerves can be felt wriggling around, sending signals to his brain, registering their survival. The pain is strong and unbearable. Becoming thicker, the mist slowly moves around Matthew's body and with it travels the ice-cold, stinging sensation. The pain is so intense. It feels as though someone is spraying liquid nitrogen everywhere this vicious energy lands.

In a desperate attempt to distract himself from the agonising pain, Matthew decides to refocus his attention on his reflection. Suddenly he notices a change in his features. His mouth begins to move ever so slightly. Again, this is completely out of his control. Matthew unexpectedly hears a voice once again. The voice is his.

"I won't lose you… Eve."

Instantly his breathing becomes heavier; his chest feels as though someone is sat on it, suppressing his lungs. Now he's in sheer panic mode.

"What have I done – where's Eve?"

Unable to answer his own questions, Matthew stares into the mirror; he's focusing all his attention on the 9mm pistol he holds so calmly in his hands. The rocking motion speeds up. He stares at his face as he rocks back and forth, his expression lifeless, until once again a movement slowly begins at his mouth. Matthew is again powerless to stop it. This time a smile appears on his face. This smile is in no way a reflection of the emotions running through his body and circulating within his mind.

As he begins to question his sanity, he sees a female silhouette appear within the mirror. Frozen with fear, Matthew stares as she gracefully moves her way around the reflection. Unable to blink, he's captivated by her image. Her features slowly begin to make an appearance. He sees her smile. She's enchanting, provocative and begins luring him into a false sense of security, distracting him from the reality of the pain he's in. Matthew's almost breathing this woman in.

"Lauren… You came back…"

Trapped in the moment, he feels an intense state of euphoria and is embracing each second of this mesmerising possession. Staring intently, he's now convinced it's Lauren. He surrenders himself to the female entity, failing to notice the progression of the mist. It's surrounding the mirror, becoming thick. Eventually it covers the mirror. Matthew becomes flustered.

"Lauren… Lauren…"

As the mist begins to ease away, the woman in the reflection suddenly leaps out of the mirror towards Matthew! She is nothing like Lauren. Jet-black long hair hangs heavy on either side of her face, dripping a black substance. Her skin is the deepest shade of grey, with deep rips scattered across it. These sinister gaping holes ooze the same black substance. As she attempts to absorb Matthew's soul with her demonic eyes, they become the deepest shade of red as her power grows stronger with every second that passes. Her lips are grey and the black substance gushes from her mouth, rolling down her chin. Matthew's heart feels as though it's about to burst at the sight of her grey, stained teeth stretching out aggressively. Forcing herself towards him, she reaches out to pull him into the mirror with her.

With a sudden *gasp* of air, Matthew leaps forward. He's soaking wet from head to toe, undressed and wearing nothing but his boxer shorts and is, once again, unexplainably back in his bed. He touches his face, his mouth, and pats his hands all over his body. Relief begins to set in as he realises it was, as Eve suggested, just a bad dream.

Collapsing back onto his pillow and breathing heavily, Matthew stares at the bright white painted walls and beings to inhale the pure air circulating around him. The bedroom window is open slightly and the fresh sea breeze is gradually blowing into the room. Embracing the safety of his home, he reaches to the bedside table and grabs the small white alarm clock. The time is flashing green. It's five thirty a.m. He falls back on the pillow to rest. No sooner has his sight adjusted to the fact that he's home than he sees something that makes his eyes protrude from their sockets.

Matthew is sure he made the transition from nightmare to reality, yet here he lies in shock. Once again unable to move, he's stuck. His eyes tell no lies. Matthew sees the shadowy woman in the corner of his room, staring directly at him. Matthew sees this isn't the Lauren he remembered at all. Placing her grey, lacerated forefinger firmly to her mouth, she mimes, "Shh…"

Matthew opens his mouth in a desperate attempt to scream, but no sound comes out. He blinks and suddenly she disappears. Still unable to speak, he lies there in a panic. Before he can come to terms with what has just transpired, she returns! Except this time, she's closer than ever and sat on the side of his bed.

Seeing her true form, the reality of her horrific presence, Matthew remains in disbelief. With her head low, she's facing towards the window and is dripping the same mysterious black substance all over his bed.

She sits still, as if she's feeding from the fear radiating off his soul and gaining strength with every second that passes. Matthew lies paralysed with terror. Tears begin to fall down his motionless face.

She rises off the bed. Matthew doesn't move. He's holding his breath. For a brief moment, he believes the evil entity is about to disappear. Standing with her back turned to him, she has once again lured him into a false sense of security.

She turns and throws out her arms to grab Matthew.

"Help!" Matthew screams.

As the word leaves his mouth her demonic features flash close to his face.

Then, thankfully, she's gone.

CHAPTER NINE

New Eyes

As the car pulls up in front of the huge steel school gates, Eve looks across to her dad.

"Are you sure you're okay? You've been very quiet this morning, Dad."

"Yes, darling, I'm fine. Please don't start worrying about me." Leaning over and tucking his daughter's hair behind her ears, he continues, "I'm lucky I have you, Evelyn Jade Honey."

Taking in the moment, Matthew lives each individual second as though he runs the risk of never having the privilege again. Smiling back, Eve seems satisfied with her dad's response. She turns to get out of the car.

"Darling, where's your mum's necklace?"

"It's here," she immediately replies.

"Sorry, panicked for a second then. I couldn't see it."

"Dad, maybe you shouldn't go into work today. I think you need time out." Pausing she then says, "I mean after all, it is Friday, I could just stay with you and we could start the weekend early. What do you think?"

Smirking at her attempt to get a day off school, Matthew sternly responds, "I'm fine. Now go on, get into school before you're late."

Jumping out the car, Eve shouts, "Love ya."

With her final words, she slams the car door shut. Matthew sits watching his daughter walking off in a world of her own. As Eve enters the school gates, he notices a group of girls closely following her. Their intentions seem impure and they appear to be laughing and mocking Eve behind her back.

Four young pretty girls, each with long blonde hair. They're walking along in perfect synchronisation with one another. They hold matching handbags over their shoulders, matching grey socks are pulled up to their knees and they all wear make-up that has been perfectly painted on their faces. All four of them are pointing, laughing and pulling spiteful facial expressions. Rage builds up inside of Matthew. He's now completely unable to control his emotions. He gets out of the car and shouts across to the girls, "Oi, you lot, leave it out."

The girls turn around to see who has just shouted.

Not content with the warning words he has shouted, he makes his way around the front of the car. The girls jump as they realise who's yelling. He recognises one of the young girls.

"Stacey, don't think I won't have a word with your dad!" he yells.

Eve turns back at the sound of her dad's voice. She turns red with embarrassment, puts her head down and runs through the huge dark-oak double doors.

The girls all blush too. They've been caught out. They scurry off with their heads down, whispering to one another.

Matthew looks around and sees all the astonished faces of the young adults making their way to school.

"Show's over," he shouts.

He storms back to the car, gets in and places his head on the steering wheel. Adrenaline races throughout his mind and body. Matthew closes his eyes and takes deep breaths, desperately attempting to regain control of his emotions once more. Focusing on the purity of the air he breathes so deeply, he begins to embrace it, feeling alive. Matthew's thoughts begin to drift.

Suddenly he sees a flashback of the demonic woman. He shakes the traumatic vision out of his mind. As he opens his eyes he shudders.

"It was just a bad dream."

Looking up, he stares at the clear blue sky. The serenity of nature helps to calm his thoughts and soothe his mind. The world appears bright and the freedom of the birds gracefully flying free gives him a sense of empowerment.

Attempting to shift his mood back into his usual, happy vibration, Matthew smiles and turns up the stereo. His favourite chill-out collection is playing through the speakers. Feeling slightly more relaxed than before, he is confident that he can start the weekend with a positive mind-set. And so, with his new eyes and gratitude for life, Matthew shakes off his fears and begins driving to work.

As he pulls up to the entrance of the huge gravel car park at the Honey Productions offices, the morning sun is shining its brightest. The security staff lift the barrier.

"Thank you."

"You're welcam', Mr Honey, and gud mornin' to you," a slightly Jamaican voice says through the speaker.

"Good morning, Eric."

Matthew finds a spot and parks up. He sees himself as equal to everyone who works at the company, all eighty-seven of them. Parking is on a first come, first serve basis. The only parking rule is that all staff must park their vehicles alongside one another. Matthew strongly believes that first impressions count. Reaching into the side of the car door, he grabs his phone and places it inside his silk-lined pocket. He picks up his briefcase and, for a moment, sits back. Taking his phone back out of his pocket, he checks his messages. There are multiple missed calls and messages from various people, but Matthew has not one missed call or even a message from the one person whose name he desires to see: Jess. With disappointment and confusion fast spreading across his face, he pulls up Jess's contact number.

"Where did you go?"

Matthew remains deep in thought for a moment.

Suddenly, he feels a slight sense of guilt for losing his cool this morning and embarrassing his daughter. He decides to text Eve:

Darling, I'm sorry.

As he steps out of the car and walks towards the building, he makes a mental note of the registration plates of the cars neatly lined up in the car park. He smiles. Matthew knows exactly who's in the office. He enters the high-rise, brown brick building through the rotating glass doors. The simple external structure belies the magnificence of the interior. As soon as you enter, you're greeted by huge silver letters that spell out "Honey Productions", centrally positioned and standing proud. With Lauren's irreplaceable stamp all over it, the interior design of this building is unique. In the entrance area, there are several identical meeting rooms, divided by glass partitions. Each room has a glistening red door with a black long modern handle. Inside, there is a long glass table, surrounded by ten high-back red leather chairs. The rooms also all have a seventy-two inch flatscreen television positioned on a white cabinet. At present, all of the meeting rooms are occupied. Honey Productions is extremely busy. People are buzzing around the building. Making his way towards the oversized curved glass reception desk, Matthew is greeted by his charming, friendly and often hyper receptionist, Daniel.

"Good morning, Matthew."

"Good morning, Daniel. Any messages for me?"

"Yes, you've got an urgent call from Mr Hews. Erm, something about voiceover issues. Then, another from Vera, Bill Hades's PA. She wants you to call her back when you get the chance. What else was it? Oh, damn… erm." Tapping a pencil on his head, Daniel tries to remember the final message. "I'm sure I wrote it down somewhere…"

"I tell you what, email me."

"Okay, will do, Matthew."

Grabbing a newspaper and placing it under his arm, Matthew makes his way over to the glass lift and presses the button. As he waits patiently for the lift's arrival, Daniel shouts one final message.

"Ah ha, found it. A lady called Jess rang for you this morning. Let me see, let me see, nope, she didn't leave a message, just a name."

Matthew immediately heads back to Daniel.

"Jess?"

Pausing, Daniel looks at his notepad and begins quickly flicking through the pages.

"Yes, erm, she said her name was Jess but, she didn't want to leave a message."

"Are you sure she didn't say anything else, anything at all?"

Confused by Matthew's reaction, Daniel replies, "No."

"Erm, it's okay, I'm sure she'll call back."

Matthew then makes his way back to the lift. Hearing a *ding* as the glass lift arrives, he steps in, presses five, and as the doors close he shuts his eyes. Now alone with his thoughts, Matthew feels an overwhelming surge of guilt.

He leans his back against the glass, and without warning the memory of a very significant event appears in his mind. His eyes remain closed and he smiles.

It's Matthew wedding day. The room is white, fresh and he's surrounded by orange and yellow flowers that create a radiant glow. Standing tall in his navy-blue suit, the only sound he can hear is each deep breath he takes as he waits in anticipation for the arrival of his soul mate. Beaming brighter than the stars, he is the proudest man alive. Not once in the lead up to the wedding has he experienced nerves; he can't wait to commit his life to Lauren.

Matthew sees the giant mahogany doors begin to open. With his hands placed behind his back, he looks down and takes a deep breath in and, as he raises his head, there she is. Standing strong and beaming with pride in her white lace, fitted wedding dress, is his soul mate. Her smile is brighter than the stars. Tears of pride, tears of joy and tears of love fall down his face as she gracefully glides down the aisle, making her way towards him.

Matthew once again hears *ding* as the lift arrives at his floor. He feels the floor bounce slightly, bringing him out of his vision and sadly back into his reality.

Regaining his posture, he steps out of the lift and begins to walk past the desks of his colleagues, greeting each of them with a smile.

"Good morning, Matthew."

"Good morning, Sarah."

"Good morning, Mr Honey."

"Ha-ha, good morning, Jack. What have I told you? Matthew is fine."

"Sorry, Mr Honey, I mean – Matthew."

"Good morning, Matthew. I've sent you an email regarding filming at the Tattoo Convention in Surrey."

"Good morning, Esme. Oh, that's great, thank you. Did you manage to get some quality footage for me?"

"Yeah, oh my God, the event was great. Just you wait till you see what me and James captured on camera. You're gonna be jealous that you didn't go."

"Ha-ha, I'm sure I will. Thanks again for covering for me at such short notice."

"No problem, just don't you go forgetting my Christmas bonus."

"Never would."

Smiling, Matthew approaches his office. He unlocks the door and as he's about to enter, he's stopped.

"Matthew, is everything okay?"

"Morning, Christina. Yeah, sure, why'd you ask?"

"Well, Eve sent a text to Melissa the other night, suggesting she was going to…" She lowers her tone. "End it all. She only just told me this morning when I drove her to school. I thought she'd been acting weird, recently but I just assumed it was, you know, that time of the month."

"Oh, Christina, I'm so sorry, yeah Eve's fine now. Well, I say now… what it was… well, I… erm, keep this to yourself."

"I promise."

"I actually got chatting to a woman the other day."

"A woman! Matthew, really?"

"Yes, a woman, shh, keep ya voice down. Well, I invited her for tea and after that pretty much the rest is a blur."

"How was Eve about it? Do you need me to talk to her?"

"At first she was horrified. Actually, she was furious. And then, strangely enough, she was, I think, just fine with it."

"Matthew, what do you mean, you think?"

"Listen, Christina, you wouldn't believe me even if I told you. Thanks for letting me know, I'll have a chat with her later. You busy today?"

"Well, I'm here if you need me. I'll let Melissa know in a minute, she's been worried sick about her. Nope, not particularly busy today, just passing through to try and book some new appointments and check my emails."

"New appointments, that's what I like to hear. You and Lauren always were the twin sister queens of sales."

"Ha-ha, you know this. See you later."

"See you later. Oh, tell Dave *the rave* I said hey."

Matthew enters his office and places his briefcase down on the floor at the side of the two-seater black leather couch next to the doorway. Walking over to his solid oak desk, as he places the newspaper down he notices the light on his office phone is flashing. He presses the hands-free button and play.

"You have three new messages and seven saved messages. To listen to new messages, press one. To listen—"

Matthew interrupts and presses one. He makes his way to the window, placing his hands behind his back. The voicemail messages begin playing out.

"First message received today at seven forty-five a.m. *Beep*. Matthew, it's Bill, call me when you get this. *Beep*.

"Second message received today at seven fifty-eight a.m. *Beep*. Hi, Matthew, it's Laura calling from TLC Operatives, could you please check the edits I've sent across to you? Many thanks. *Beep*.

"Final message received today at eight thirty-six a.m. *Beep*. Hi, Matthew. It's Vera, Bill Hades's PA, can you give me a call when you get this, please? Many thanks. *Beep*.

"End of messages. To listen to these messages again, press one."

Making his way over to his desk, Matthew lifts the receiver and puts it down to end the call.

As he peers out of the huge window from the fifth floor, he's surprisingly disappointed. Matthew thought at least one of the messages might have been from Jess. Standing alone with his thoughts, he hears chitter chatter and laughter coming from his colleagues outside his office; he smiles at their happiness. Reaching into his pocket he pulls out the piece of paper containing the number Daniel wrote down and walks over to his desk. Much like his home, the layout is immaculate and not a single item leans so much as a centimetre out of place. Putting the piece of paper containing Jess's number down, he peers across to the family photograph of him, Lauren and Eve. Suddenly he feels an overwhelming surge of sadness.

"God only knows how much I miss you."

No sooner has he spoken these words than Matthew feels his phone vibrating inside his pocket. He pulls it out and sees Jess's name flashing like a strobe light. Before he knows it, he's answering the call.

"Hello, Matthew Honey speaking."

"I was worried about you."

He smiles.

Eve sits at the front of the class in her English lesson. She's daydreaming about nothing of any significance when suddenly her teacher, Ms Phelps, *bangs* a book on her desk. She jumps with fright, the unexpected movement shifting her back into reality.

Eve flicks through the pages, desperately trying to work out where the class are up to. English isn't her favourite subject. She considers herself a creative, free spirit, and it doesn't help that Ms Phelps is extremely strict. She believes children should only be seen and never heard. Ms Phelps's classroom has the same eerie energy as her gloomy appearance. She looks as though she has never been loved and gets dressed in the dark every day. Lipstick is always plastered across her teeth. This isn't her only unattractive trait; she always has an overbearing stench of coffee breath. It's disgusting. During Ms Phelps's classes, pupils are *not* permitted to speak unless she authorises them to do so.

"Now, in complete silence. That means *no* reading out loud. I want you all to read the following highlighted passages on your worksheets. Make notes on the grammatical errors, as I will be testing you on this in the next five minutes, before the end of class."

There's a sudden tap on the window of the classroom door and Ms Phelps leaves the room. Once the door's shut and Ms Phelps is out of sight, Eve hears mocking words and laughter coming from the girls at the back of the class. It's the same group of cruel girls who were taunting her this morning.

"Oh, my name's Eve. I get my daddy to stick up for me."

"Ha-ha, yeah, even though I'm a murderer and I killed my mum."

"I know, he probably doesn't even know he's next. Am I right, girls? Ha-ha."

The girls all laugh loudly, satisfied with their bullying intentions.

"Enough!" Eve shouts, her head down.

Ms Phelps immediately bursts back into the room.

"Evelyn Honey, how dare you shout in my classroom!"

Eve, the girl who would normally cower away and hide in the corner crying until her eyes were sore, is now the complete opposite. Much like her dad earlier, she's unable to control her emotions. Unable to stop the rage from growing inside of her. The pencil she holds in her hand snaps. Sharp shards of wood penetrate her skin and blood slowly drips out. Completely oblivious to this, Eve digs the pencil further into the palm of her hand. As her fury grows, her grip gets tighter. Eve's chest begins pulsating up and down as her breathing rapidly increases. Her eyes suddenly become overcast. As this new energy takes over each blood vessel, her sight has been overpowered, and her eyes are now jet-black. Not a patch of white can be seen. Her head remaining down, Eve thinks of one thing only. Her mind and all her energy are completely focused on the girls at the back of the class.

The girls simultaneously place their hands over their ears, pressing them tightly. It's as though they're desperately attempting to block out sound, but no sound can be heard within the walls of the classroom. Each girl has a pained expression on her face and they all start screeching at the tops of their voices. This group of cruel bullying girls, who ordinarily feed from the evil energy they all share, now look vulnerable. No longer do they look as though they should be feared. No longer do they look strong. These bitchy cruel girls are weakened, as their minds are being taken over by the unknown.

All the other pupils in the classroom panic, jumping from their chairs. Most of them don't look back and leave their belongings. Once every single innocent pupil has frantically burst out of the classroom, a gust of wind begins to blow. The heavy brown door bangs and the door locks itself. The girls, now curled up on the floor, are still covering their ears as they screech louder than ever, one after the other.

The view from the window of the classroom is no longer bright and clear. Deep grey clouds materialise, and the outside world appears to be within complete darkness. Much like the storm forming outside, the angrier Eve gets, the darker the mist in her jet-black eyes becomes. Gripping the pencil, she holds tightly onto the table, then begins to drag it towards her.

From nowhere, the horrific demonic grey lady appears behind Eve. Her long jet-black hair hangs heavy. With eyes the deepest shade of blood-red, her grey sinful face is impure and terrifying. A sinister black substance drips from the deep cracks surrounding her mouth. Leaning over Eve's shoulder, this evil entity embraces every second of her possession over this young girl.

As the possession takes hold and Eve accepts it, her body is no longer pure. Her rage builds and she's unaware that she's surrendering to the desires of the demonic creature. A tiny section of her soul is being retained and locked deep within this evil entity's deceitful black heart. Her black heart that no longer beats. Her black heart that oozes neglect and supremacy. While it holds this carefully selected soul captive, this same unnerving organ is now absorbing Eve's DNA, making them connect as one. Now there's no going back.

As if drawn by a magnetic pull, they stand close together. Eve feels the demonic woman's breath brushing past her skin. Each exhale is freezing cold. The sinister black substance that drips from the cracks surrounding her mouth begins to gush forth as she separates her lips. Leaving its sickening presence wherever it lands, the black liquid has the stench of death attached to it.

Seeming content with her control over Eve, she spits out the thick black bloody substance and begins whispering directly into her ear, "Ring a' Ring o' Roses – your soul is mine."

Eve instantly stands, and with a sudden twitch of her head, the girls who remain in agony on the floor now move their hands around their own throats. They gasp and struggle for air as they begin choking. Eve turns and makes her way towards the back of the class. With every step closer Eve gets to the girls, they struggle to fight for their lives.

Ms Phelps, frozen with fear, watches the disturbing unnatural events unfold. This strong, overpowering woman has, much like the cruel bullying girls, lost her voice. Like a statue, she stands at the blackboard next to the book cabinet by the doorway. Ms Phelps, unfortunately, didn't make it out of the classroom before the door was locked. She is being forced to watch the events taking place against her own will. There is not so much as a twitch of her facial features.

Reaching the girls, Eve bends down. Her eyes are so black they form mirrors, showing a reflection of the desperate girls. Uncontrollably choking and unable to beg for release, each girl has fear plastered across her face. As their own hands tighten around their necks, their eyes begin to protrude from their sockets. The struggle to breathe gets too much and the lack of oxygen to the brain begins taking its toll; their eyes start to roll slowly towards the back of their heads. Eve's now satisfied with their suffering and, just as they're all about to pass out, she leans across and says, "*Ti libero per ora.*"

The girls, along with Ms Phelps, who falls to the floor, instantly lose consciousness.

The demonic evil entity looks satisfied at Eve's ability to receive commands and willingly surrender. Making her way over to Eve, she leans to her ear once more and whispers, "Welcome to the dark side."

With her final words spoken, the evil entity disappears. Eve stands. The girls remain in the same position. They are motionless and silent on the floor. Their eyes are wide open, bright red and swollen. A faint line begins to appear on the surface of the skin around their necks. As the oxygen once again circulates around their bodies, this faint line develops a deep red bruised tone, leaving the mark of strangulation on their skin.

Feeling a sense of euphoria at this confirmation of her bullies' intense suffering, Eve calmly makes her way back towards her desk, collects her belongings and walks towards the classroom door. With every step she takes, her eyes slowly revert to their normal tone. As the mist leaves her eyes, the intense effect of the possession leaves Eve's body.

Making no attempt to look back, Eve steps over Ms Phelps and glances down at the bullying teacher. Lay in a trance-like state, Ms Phelps is flat on her back, with her head facing up. Her eyes are wide open, but you can see she lacks full consciousness. This once strong woman is frozen with fear. She looks as though her soul has left its physical form as a tear slowly ventures down her motionless face.

"Scordatelo," Eve says with a smirk on her face.

With her command made, Eve feels empowered. She is certain there will be no repercussions to her actions. The door then unlocks. Content with her actions, Eve exits the classroom, leaving the aftermath behind her. As she steps out onto the corridor, she closes the door. The hallway is still and quiet, not a single person can be seen. As the bell begins ringing loudly throughout the school, Eve places her backpack over her shoulder and makes her way towards the front entrance. Her eyes are now, once again, her own. Laughing as she skips down the steps, Eve once again says, *"Scordatelo."*

CHAPTER TEN

Suspicious or Paranoid?

"Table for two, usual spot, please."

Matthew is standing next to the island in the kitchen on the phone to his favourite Italian restaurant. "Time? Eight thirty. Brilliant, thanks Daniela, see you then." He ends the call and straightaway makes another.

"Hi, Jess. Yes, it's all booked. So, I'll meet you out front. Shall we say twenty past eight?" He continues, "Great, I look forward to it. See you later, alligator."

Putting the phone down, Matthew says, "Alligator, what the f—"

Shaking his head and laughing to himself, he places the phone into his pocket, turns and makes his way towards the day room. Now home from school, Matthew sees Eve sitting on the couch with her feet tucked up. The television is blaring. She's laughing away at her favourite American TV show, *Friends*. Walking over to the couch, he sits right beside his daughter.

"Oh, is this the one where Monica has a cold?"

"Yeah, I'm in the *pribe ob libe*. Ha-ha. Classic."

Laughing, Matthew pulls Eve in tight. Kissing her on the head he whispers, "I love you, darling."

Eve smiles as she looks up at her dad.

"Love you too, Dad."

"You will always be my priority. My number one and my right-hand lady, no matter what, I will *always* take care of you."

"I know, Dad."

Eve begins to snuggle her dad tight. The silence says it all, and both father and daughter enjoy the moment together and settle in to watch the TV. Eve is in a world of her own, giggling away. Matthew looks at his watch. He has four hours before his date with Jess. Glancing out of the huge window he sees the sun's shinning and the tide is still out. Turning to Eve, he says, "Fancy a walk along the beach with me, kidda?"

"Sure, but why… Hang on, what's going on?"

"You're always suspicious, Evelyn Jade." Laughing, he continues, "Honestly, it's nothing, I promise."

"Hmm…"

"Look – I cross my heart. I just thought it would be nice to go for a walk along the beach together. Clear mind's a healthy mind."

"Okay, then, lemme just get my jacket."

Matthew and Eve walk hand in hand along the beach front, quietly enjoying each other's company. The huge grey and white seagulls are on top form this evening as they circle above them. Once of these magnificent but greedy birds realise Matthew and Eve serve them no purpose, as they have no food in their hands, they quickly fly off looking for anyone who might be able to feed them.

The waves slowly break, one after the other. The sound of this is calming. Not too far out in the distance you can see the outlines of the boats as they gently float on the water. Matthew stops walking and stretches out his arms. He takes in the biggest deep breath, filling his lungs.

"You feel that, darling?"

"Huh…"

"This is what being alive feels like in one single moment. Try it."

Eve laughs as she copies her dad's actions.

Matthew smells the fresh salty sea water. It feels as if it is cleansing his lungs, enhancing his sense of true inner happiness.

"Feels good. Am I right, kidda?"

Laughing, she replies, "Suppose so."

"You know something? The minute you were placed into my arms, I looked at you and I couldn't believe it. I had gifted this beautiful little girl with life. Okay, your perfection is mainly from your mum's genetics, but nonetheless, you are half me, too."

Eve smiles. She grabs her dad's hand, then suddenly winces and lets go.

"You all right, darling?"

"Yes, sorry. I hurt myself at school today and cut my hand. It just hurts a little, that's all."

"Here, let me take a look at it." Matthew says as he pulls Eve's hand towards him, "How did you do that?" he says shocked.

Pulling her hand back, Eve says, "Erm, I don't really remember. Honestly, I'm fine. Come on."

Grabbing her dad's hand once more, Eve drags him closer to the water.

"Eve… What are you doing?"

"Just shut up and run with me."

Dipping her hands into the freezing cold sea water, she cups them and chucks a handful directly at her dad. It splashes him in the face.

"Oh, really – so you wanna play, do you kidda? Right, well it's game on."

Matthew starts laughing and mirrors her actions. The pair, now behaving like innocent children, begin having a water fight. Passers-by laugh as they look on at the fun and joy they are creating. The dogs playing freely on the beach hear the laughter and run over, ready to join in the fun. They bark with excitement and wag their tails, wanting desperately to play.

Matthew's still got his suit on, making this family-fun snapshot even more picture perfect. Giggling away, Eve creates waves, splashing water in her dad's direction. They're both soaking wet, but radiating love, joy and happiness. Eventually, accepting defeat and running away somewhat theatrically, Matthew heads back towards the manmade, grey brick wall. Eve's not too far behind him. She shouts, "Come back, you wimp."

Seemingly out of breath, Matthew rests on the low wall with his hands in the air.

"I give up. You win."

"Yes. I win. I'm a winner, Dad!"

Laughing, they both sit side by side, staring out at the tranquil surroundings. This is home. This is where they belong. Taking off his jacket and placing it on the wall to dry, Matthew grabs Eve and tucks her under his soggy arm.

"Eww."

"You know something, kidda, when I went to see your mum in the Chapel of Rest, I made a commitment to her. Have I ever told you this story?"

"No, go on, what did you say?"

"I made a commitment that I would never let you go. Her sacrifice would be my strength to protect you always in life and, if for any reason I lost you, I vowed that I would never rest, and I would search the ends of the earth to find you."

"Aww, Dad, that's so sweet. But honestly, I'm going nowhere."

"I spoke to your Auntie Christina today at work. Melissa is very worried about you."

"Oh. Now I understand. Dad, look, I'm sorry, I didn't mean it. Well, I did in that moment. I was at Mum's 'Garden of Secrets' and I was just so mad. But, I'm fine with it."

"Eve, I have something to say, I'm—"

"I know," Eve interrupts. "Go on your date with Jess. Like I said, I'm fine with it. I just want you to be happy, Dad."

Matthew smiles, "Are you sure, kidda? You would tell me if it got too much? You're always my priority."

"I know, Dad, it's fine. I like Jess, she's all right. When I'm around her, it's weird, she kinda makes me feel… what's the word I'm looking for… that's it, she makes me feel empowered."

Tapping her on the head gently, he says, "Erm… Hello… Can I have my Eve back, please? Clearly this is an imposter. I'll never understand women. You all literally confuse the life out of me."

Standing in the cold but extremely organised garage, Matthew's frantically searching for something, reaching high on the shelves and pulling out the contents of drawers, cabinets, boxes and everything else in his proximity. Matthew scratches his head.

"I'm sure it is here somewhere."

He grabs a box from the highest shelf.

"Ah ha, found it."

He holds firmly in his hand an immaculate box containing two micro-sized cameras. Being a professional film-maker and technology nerd has its perks; he always has the latest cameras and gadgets. Taking the box up to his bedroom, he places its contents on the bedside table: two teeny tiny cameras. He holds them in his hands, trying to work out where to put them. His mind begins to drift and he starts to wonder if he's actually being overly paranoid.

Putting cameras up in the house, really? It's a bit extreme, Matthew. After all, it's only a bad dream.

Yes, but these dreams have been severe enough to have me questioning my reality. There's no harm in putting them up. What's the worst that can happen? You'll either see something or you won't. No-one needs to know, and no harm done.

His mind wants answers and it looks as though this is the only logical way he's going to receive them. He sets about placing one of the cameras at the end of his curtain pole in his bedroom. The other, he places on the corner of a picture frame inside Eve's bedroom. These wireless genius inventions cannot be seen by the naked eye.

If this demonic woman is real, or if she isn't, and Matthew is, in fact, just experiencing nightmares through guilt, then the cameras won't lie. But maybe, just maybe, something strange is going on and the cameras will confirm it. What if Lauren *is* revisiting him in the night? What if she's expressing her disgust at him bringing another woman into Eve's life, or what if he is losing his mind? Either way, the outcome for him would be one of great intensity, and Matthew's extremely nervous about the result. He's even more nervous about the outcome of this than he is about his date with Jess, which is now less than one hour away.

Matthew stands outside the entrance of the restaurant, in his favourite navy-blue suit, white shirt, and navy-blue bow tie, looking as handsome as ever. His hair is slicked back and tiny deep silver strands peer through the slight curls on either side. He's waiting in great anticipation for the arrival of his date. He looks at his watch, and as he peers back up, she's there. He is speechless. Walking across to the taxi, he opens the car door. With elegance Jess places one foot after the other and steps out.

"Why, thank you, Mr Honey."

He hands the taxi driver payment for the journey, then turns and sees her clearly. She's wearing a floor-length red dress with lace beautifully detailed around the neckline and down the sleeves. A silver glisten can be seen from the locket that hangs close to her chest. Her thick brown hair is styled to perfection, sitting over her shoulders. It flows ever so gently in the breeze. Jess's eyes are radiant and enchanting; so enchanting, in fact, Matthew finds himself locked into her sight. With utter admiration, and a trance-like expression upon his face, he says: "You really are so very beautiful."

Matthew's completely unaware of the awkward silence he's once again creating.

"Shall we?" Jess says.

"Yes, erm, sorry, after you."

As they enter the romantic, rustic restaurant, they smell the fresh bread, pizzas and tomato-based sauces cooking. This fabulous restaurant is family run. Authentic Italian music plays gently in the background and multiple pictures with fairy lights can be seen hanging on the walls, giving all their customers a true taste of Italy.

They wait for a moment in the beautifully lit and warming reception area before being shown to their table for the evening by their server, Daniela.

"Ciao, Mr Honey, so good to always be seeing you again. I will be your server for this evening. If you will be needing anything, please let me know. I am always being happy to be helping you, and your beautiful lady friend." He passes them both a menu. "Today we have the specials for you, a calzone of your choosing, ravioli, mussels, fillet steak pepe and polo crème. I will leave you to browse at your timing, but can I be getting you any drinks in the meantime?"

"I've got this," Matthew says. "Daniela, we'll have your best bottle of rosé wine, please."

"I'm impressed that you remembered, Mr Honey."

Matthew's feeling slightly proud of himself, as this is probably the only thing he can remember from the time they spent together. His ego collects the brownie points he has just been rewarded. Matthew and Jess smile in sync as they look down at their menus.

"Out of interest, what is your favourite place to eat out?" Matthew asks.

But before she has chance to answer, Daniela approaches the table with their wine. Pouring it into their glasses, he explains, "This is a Chateau d'Esclans, Les Clans and Garrus, from the Esclans range. This is our most popular of the rosé wines."

"Thank you," Jess says as she reaches out with her left hand and takes her wine glass. She begins swirling it and smells the wine.

"You're left-handed?"

"Yes…"

He sits back in total disbelief. "Lauren was left-handed." He laughs. "How did I not notice? So similar, this is just weird."

"Really? I would never have known. How peculiar."

Jess looks to Matthew and, as she places her wine glass back on the table, she says, "In answer to your question, I don't really have a favourite place to eat. You see, I'm fairly new to the area and so I'm unsure of the best places, or indeed any places, to eat out at."

"Oh, really? So where are you from, then?"

"Well now, here's a question for you, Mr Honey. Would you, in fact, like to know where I am from, or where I currently live?"

"Erm, I've never been asked that question before. But, well, I guess I'd like to know… Hmm, can I say both?"

Laughing, she responds, "Of course you can. I just wasn't too sure if you were interested. Well, I'm originally from a small village called Gehenna."

"I've never heard of it."

"You never will, it's a very small village. Now, Mr Honey, I live wherever I desire."

"So, you're homeless then?" Matthew laughs.

"Do I look homeless?"

"No, sorry, I was joking," he says, embarrassed.

"You're lucky I like you, Mr Honey. You're forgiven. I meant it metaphorically. I am what's known as a free spirit."

Taking out his phone, Matthew says, "Gehenna, you say. How are you spelling that, is it G—"

Before he has time to finish, Jess takes the phone from out of his hand and erases the internet search he was about to complete.

"No phones this evening, Mr Honey. I want your full attention to be on me."

"Please, call me Matthew. So, come on then, enlighten me, how come Eve's now your biggest fan?" He places his hand on his head. "What did I miss while I was out of it?"

"I told you I would empower her. You see, Matthew, I know how the complicated mind of a teenage girl works."

"Me too, I was a teenage girl once too, you know."

Laughing awkwardly, Jess replies, "Ha-ha, yes, you are funny, aren't you?"

Coughing as though he's clearing his throat, when he's actually trying to distract from the discomfort he's created, Matthew says, "Really, though, I'd seriously like to thank you."

"Thank me?"

"Yes, whatever you've said to Eve has made a huge difference; she seems calm again. I can only imagine it's your influence."

"Oh Matthew, don't worry, I'll always help. I'm here for Eve."

"Well, it's greatly appreciated. As you can imagine, after everything we've both been through, Eve has to be my priority, and it's a huge relief to me that she's been able to build a connection, of sorts, with you."

"You don't need to thank me for that. She's a precious soul and has the ability to be a strong, powerful woman. I can see her making an unforgettable influence on the universe. Call it a prediction."

"That's very kind of you to say."

"I only speak words of truth."

It's Friday evening and the restaurant is packed. The Italian music is playing gently in the background, and as Matthew's beginning to relax, the conversation develops from awkward to engaging. The pair begin to resemble flirty innocent school kids. The smiles, the giggles and the chemistry begin to show. As the night progresses, they're both enjoying each other's company so much that there might as well be a spotlight on their table and everyone else frozen in time.

CHAPTER ELEVEN

It's... Showtime!

As Matthew and Jess arrive back at the house, they see Eve making her way down the stairs and heading in their direction.

"Hey, darling. Look who's come to say hello."

Bypassing her dad, she makes her way across to Jess like a magnet and without saying a single word, she stands directly by her side.

"Aye, kidda, where's my hug?"

Standing with her head held high, Jess looks pleased by Eve's seemingly impulsive action.

"It's so lovely to see you again, Eve. I've had a wonderful evening with your father. It's a shame you couldn't join us."

Eve says nothing. Her expression is blank as she peers up at Jess. She is yet to make any form of contact with her dad.

"Erm, earth to Eve."

She turns to her dad. "Hello, Dad," she says. Her voice sounds broken and robotic.

"Hello, Eve. What's gotten into you...?"

Not only does Eve choose to ignore her dad's question, she turns back to look at Jess as though he doesn't exist.

"What the f—You avin' a laugh?" Puzzled, he continues, "Kidda, tell you what, it's getting late, time for you to head to bed."

Jess and Eve maintain strong eye contact. Suddenly, Jess gently nods her head. Without any warning or sound, Eve makes her way across to her dad, kisses him and heads up the stairs.

"Shall we have a nightcap?" Jess says, as if nothing has happened.

Matthew follows her into the kitchen, confused. "Hang about, what was that?"

"What was what?"

"That, just then – that with Eve?"

"I don't know what you're referring to, Mr Honey."

"Jess, don't try to mug me off. And it's Matthew. You know exactly what I'm on about. My daughter just ignored me like I don't exist."

"She didn't. Matthew, you're over-reacting."

"*My* daughter hasn't walked past me like that for a long time."

"So, what you're saying is, we can't win with you? Eve no longer gets angry at my presence and this – what – angers you? Shouldn't you just be happy that we're getting along?" Walking across to Matthew, Jess wraps her arms around his neck. "Matthew, I don't know the answer. Maybe Eve's drawn to me because she has not had female company since her mum died. Maybe she has just missed having a woman around."

Pushing her away, Matthew is in shock and unconvinced by Jess's words.

"I'd rather you didn't speak about Lauren like that. She may be gone in body, but she's still very much a big part of our lives."

"Matthew, relax. Here, drink this," she says, passing him the glass of wine she has just poured. "I told you, I'm here for Eve. We've had a lovely evening. Do you really want to spoil our time together because *your* daughter actually likes me?"

Sipping his wine and thinking about what just happened, Matthew begins to slowly surrender. Although it pains him to admit it, he knows she's right. With a hint of embarrassment, he submissively reverts back to his usual understanding and rational thinking self.

"Jess, I'm sorry, it just took me by surprise. I'm not used to seeing her so distant from me. After everything we've both been through… it made us stronger. We've been forced to adapt to our new family dynamic, just me and Eve against the world. I suppose I've gotten so used to not having to share her with anyone. I lost my train of thought for a moment. I'm sorry."

"I know it's probably strange for you, and Matthew, these moments are going to happen; I ask you just to please take them with a pinch of salt. She's a daddy's girl and I'm sure deep down she always will be. Eve must have been happy to see me. I think it's a great step in the right direction."

"I really appreciate that, and once again, I'm sorry, and I thank you for being so understanding. I truly don't know what came over me."

"It's my pleasure. You're just being a protective father, which I respect. I expect you to be that way, it's all new to you both." Leaning in, she says, "But believe me when I say your family dynamic was worth the decades of waiting."

The beachfront is dark and still. You can no longer see the outlines of the boats in the distance. Night's beginning to fall. The glisten from the street lights can be seen as they start flickering on in the growing darkness. Standing on the balcony with a glass of wine, Jess looks out at the tranquil sea. The waves are breaking gently, and the breeze is calm as the tide has now come in. The view is serene, just like the comforting energy surrounding them. Matthew stands by Jess's side and places his chin on her shoulder.

"This is my favourite time of day."

There's not one person present, not even a bird in the sky. Gazing at the small cluster of stars above, Matthew listens to the soothing sound of the sea, enjoying Jess's company.

"Can I ask you something?" Matthew says, turning to face Jess.

"Of course."

"Why are you here? I don't mean that the way it sounds. What I actually mean is, why haven't you run a mile? My life must seem chaotic to you. What makes you stick around?"

Jess remains silent for a brief moment and appears to be deep in thought, staring out at the darkness of the night.

"Do you like to play games, Matthew?"

"What sort of games?"

"Games that strengthen your mind."

"I suppose."

"Well, when you play, let's say, a board game, you have your piece and you move around the board. Yes?"

"Yes."

"Well, when you play any game, you don't know the outcome, and it's exciting, do you agree?"

"Yeah, I suppose so."

"Well, what is it you do with your excitement?" She pauses as though she's waiting for Matthew to answer her question, but before he has time to speak, Jess continues, "It becomes your energy. You put all that enthusiasm into winning the game. The thrill of the chase enables you to focus, and *you* will literally do everything you can to win. Only you know that you're not going to give up. That's the way I live my life. It's like a constant game. I can predict what I desire the outcome to be. Do I always get it right? Yes. Do I always win? Most definitely. I'm a winner, Matthew."

"So, I don't understand... What's that got to do with why you come back and don't run a mile?"

"You see, Matthew, Eve's precious mind is wide open. She's like a lost piece on the board, just wandering around, waiting to see the outcome of her fate. I'm the master of my mind and the leader of my board. I am here to empower her." Turning away, she continues, "Don't worry, though. You should know one important thing about me, Mr Honey, or Matthew, as you me to call you. I always take good care of my pieces."

With these words spoken, Jess turns to him and pulls his body onto hers. She locks eyes with him and whispers on Matthew's lips, "*Mi temono.*"

The mood instantly changes. There is a powerful vibrational shift in the air around them. The waves of the sea are no longer calm; they rise high and come crashing down, one after the other. This dark eerie energy is strong, overbearing. *They are not alone.* From the distance there is a sudden loud squawk. Jess and Matthew, oblivious to this, remain locked together by their sight. Her eyes become overcast with a grey mist. Matthew, now breathing her in, is unaware of the sudden changes around him.

The loud squawk sounds again and again, travelling closer with each second that passes. No sooner has this sound journeyed through their eardrums, and embedded deep into their minds, then a huge, black raven, bigger than your eyes have ever seen, circulates above them at a great height, flapping its beautiful and strong glossy wings. Matthew and Jess haven't so much as flinched. They are unaware of this magnificent and great bird, remaining totally entrapped within the moment and aware of nothing more.

Tucked in her bed, Eve is blissfully dreaming. She looks extremely angelic, sleeping with Gregg on the pillow next to her head. A deep, eerie mist slowly seeps through the cracks around the door into the room and sets about corrupting the innocent energy. The mood within the room becomes dark, gloomy and suppressive. The curtains begin to move as a breeze blows through the room.

Eve's leather-backed personal diary is in its usual position, closed flat on the desk. The mist travels past Eve as she shudders in her sleep and encircles her diary, taking over its secrets. There is a sudden gust, so forceful that the diary stands no chance of remaining closed, and is once again forced to flip open. The pages riffle, turning one after the other without any physical assistance. Eventually the paper stops fluttering and the diary lies open on a double page. The pages are covered with blue-inked scrawled writing that reads as follows:

"I thought about you a lot today. Me and dad were driving on the motorway to auntie Christina's house and we ended up driving past the place where me and you went paintballing. I started laughing to myself and dad asked what I was laughing at. So, I told him.

"I told him about the time where you were lay behind a hay stack and I was high up near the tree top. You couldn't see me, but I could see you. I heard you shout, 'Evelyn Jade, I'm going to win this game, I just know it.' Then I shouted, 'Don't be too sure, Mum,' and I shot you about five times. Dad started laughing, and he said that was one of your greatest qualities of all, your ability to have fun no matter what. He said

he wouldn't go paintballing with me. He's too scared of getting hurt. But not you, mum. You had no fear.

"The drive was very much silent after that. But I could still see you. I could still see your smile and hear your laughter. I relive the days we spent together a lot. I will never lose them, after all, it's all I have left of you.

"Don't worry, I'm looking after Dad and Gregg. I just wish I could speak to you one last time, see your smile one last time. I miss you, Mum. I miss having a mum. Someone I can go to. Someone I can share my days with. Someone to go shopping with. I miss everything about having you. I miss mum.

"You will always be my queen. I'm sorry I was your daughter; you might have lived if you had a different one."

Unaware that her true inner thoughts and emotions have been revealed, Eve remains in her peaceful state. She's oblivious to the grey mist seeping through the room. Lying face up, Eve's expression is pure. She is surrounded by the softest, white cotton bedsheets, with rose-gold detailing. This vulnerable young girl is entirely unaware of her chosen fate; not only this, she is unaware of the practicality she is soon to face. Eve's been elected for a great purpose. Selected from billions of souls. The wisely chosen "Ring a' Ring o' Roses" possessive rhyme is slowly taking over tiny sections of her soul. Carefully wrapping its evil charm and vindictive energy around her existence, each word is overpowering her identity, removing one tiny section at a time, so it is not to be detected, until the moment is perfect, and the possession is complete. But under whose control?

As the mist begins to thicken, it gradually travels towards Eve. Reaching the legs of her bed, it slowly moves up the frame and embeds itself in the wood. Rapidly, the atmosphere within the room changes. Once enlightened by innocence, once embracing purity, this very same room has now been taken over by a deceitful entity. The mist circles around Eve outside of the bedsheets, then wraps itself around her outline and travels through the gaps in the sheets. It sets about surrounding her body, which is covered only by her late mother's nightie. It forms bonds that appear to restrict Eve from moving. The mist is preparing the room for the arrival of its master, the leader of the dark fate, who has so carefully selected Eve. The Dark Empress.

Continuing the take-over, the thick grey mist now circulates around her face. Her expression is no longer pure. Her features are slowly changing. Her skin tone is being taken over. No longer natural, no longer pure, its shade is unknown to the world. Eve is changing to a light shade of grey. Her features twitch as the transition takes place. The room is now empowered by the deep and deceitful mist, ready for the arrival of its owner.

There isn't a living person in sight, not a single soul can be seen, and yet a voice can be heard very quietly in the room. The words that echo and radiate throughout the bedroom are: "*Non temere di me.*"

As the final soundwave disappears, the mist gradually begins to descend away from Eve's face. The transition has started to take place. From out of the mist a grey wounded hand appears and rests on the top of Eve's head. A quiet humming can be heard. Black blood begins to ooze from the deep rips in the hand. The humming turns to singing and the implantation of the possession begins:

"Ring a' Ring o' Roses – your soul is mine. Ring a' Ring o' Roses – you've been chosen for the dark side."

The rhyme is very gently repeated, over and over. As the tainted hand moves around Eve's face, the lyrics begin embedding and taking possession of her brain's living cells, one individual cell at a time. A dark, evil energy circulates within Eve's blood and quickly changes it to a sinister thick black substance as it fixes itself to every part of Eve's DNA. The nails of the hand travel down Eve's face. Black, razor-sharp and dirt-filled, these nails can rip the flesh from your bones with ease. As this sinister body part descends over her features the reality of the transition begins to show. Eve is no longer Eve. Her skin tone is the deepest shade of grey. Her lips are black. Deep rips begin to appear on her once innocent and beautiful face. Once formed, they begin oozing the same black substance that has taken possession of her DNA.

"Ring a' Ring o' Roses – your soul is mine. Ring a' Ring o' Roses – welcome to the dark side."

With the final lyric sung, the grey demonic hand pushes Eve's face at force and throws her into the dark abyss of her own mind.

Eve is falling slowly, surrounded by darkness. She is limp, as if her spinal cord has been removed from her body. An evil and unknown entity continues to drag Eve's innocent soul deeper and deeper. She's powerless, no longer the master of her fate. Taunted by the unknown and entirely unaware that she's sinking further and further into the abyss of her own mind, Eve is petrified.

She finally comes to stop. Eve remains completely still. She can hear only her heart beating and, as her sense of fear heightens, she can feel each individual pump as blood pulsates throughout her body. Frantically looking around, she sees there's nothing and no-one, there. She's sitting in complete darkness.

Being the brave young lady that she is, Eve shouts, "Hello?"

Suddenly, she doesn't feel alone. Breathing heavily, as her heartrate begins to speed up, she bravely shouts once more, "Who's there?"

With yet again no response, she cups her head in her hands and begins to sob. "Please, Mum, just say it's you," she says gently under her breath.

Music begins to play in the distance. It is making its way towards her. Slowly removing her hands from her face, Eve tunes in her ears. There are no lyrics, but she can hear a clear tune being played. It's "Ring a' Ring o' Roses".

No sooner had she recognised this piece of music than Eve is thrown into a flashback.

Eve stands in the corner of the day room. She can see herself as a small child. She looks around the room in amazement at all the decorations, lights and presents. Eve works out that it's Christmas day at home. The kind of Christmas day she used to share with Mum and Dad. Suddenly, she sees her mum walk into the room. Little Eve, who's sat by the tree, looks up and her face lights up with joy. Mummy has a present in her hand.

Eve runs over to her mum and goes to throw her arms around her… but passes right through her mum's body. She falls against the wall, and remembers that it's not reality, it's her memory. A deep internal sadness takes her over and tears begin to form in her eyes. She makes her way over to the tree and kneels beside her younger self. She watches as her mum picks up the excited little version of herself. Her beautiful mum, her wonderful, beautiful, life-fuelled mum places little Eve on her lap. She's ready to open her special present.

"Are you ready, my angel? Father Christmas left this one especially for you," her mum says.

"For me?"

"Yes, my angel, for you. Here you go."

Little Eve can't hold back any longer. She begins ripping the colourful and carefully crafted wrapping paper off the present. In her excitement, she throws it on the floor. Little Eve holds in her hand the most gorgeous, handcrafted wooden jewellery box. It has elegant white-gold detailing, and on the lid Eve's name has been carved into the wood with the same white-gold trimming. Her little face lights up.

"Evelyn Jade Honey, this is for you to cherish always. I made sure that Father Christmas got this especially for you to put all your treasures in. And, guess what? It's extra special. Do you want to know why, Evelyn Jade?"

"Why, Mummy?"

"Because listen…" She opens the lid of the box. A delicate, tiny ballerina appears and begins twirling around to the tune of Ring a' Ring o' Roses. "This was my favourite nursery rhyme when I was a little girl, just like you."

"Weally, Mummy?"

"Really, my angel."

Eve watches as her younger self hugs her mum tight.

"Dank you, Mummy, I wove it forever."

Eve snaps out of the happy memory, finding herself once again surrounded by darkness. Her head begins spinning round and round as she tries to work out why this is happening to her.

Matthew is struggling with the bedsheets in his sleep. His moans become louder and louder. "Why... No – wait, why are you doing this to me? Please, don't take her away from me. Noooooo..." he shouts, and suddenly wakes. He is soaking wet with sweat from head to toe. The room is dark. As he grabs the glass of water from his bedside table, he feels an unwelcoming, unnerving and eerie energy surrounding him. Placing the glass back on the side, Matthew turns; he sees Jess isn't in the bed. The light in the en-suite isn't on either. Wondering where she is, he shouts out, "Jess," but he gets nothing back.

Eventually, he climbs out of bed. He pinches himself harshly in order to make sure he's not stuck in a cruel entrapment. Slowly making his way towards the door, Matthew no longer feels alone. Suddenly a huge gust of wind blows through the room. Matthew stops.

"Jess... Eve?" Once again, he gets no reply.

He looks over his shoulder. He feels as if someone is standing right behind him. But, as soon as he turns, he sees there's no one there. Shaking his head and trying desperately not to let fear become his primary emotion, Matthew quickly makes his way over to the window to shut it. He stands back in shock and gasps. The window is already shut tight. He rushes towards the door, almost tripping over his own feet on the way. Not wanting to be a coward, Matthew calmly opens the door, and then bursts out onto the landing. Looking around, he sees no one is there.

Still feeling as though he's being accompanied by entities unknown, Matthew shudders as he slowly makes his way towards Eve's bedroom door. Placing his ear to the wood, he remains extremely still. He hears nothing but his own heart beating and is relieved. No sooner has his heartrate begun to regulate than he hears a noise coming from downstairs. Breathing in deeply, he heads towards the staircase. Every single part of his brain is sending alarm bells and telling him not to go towards the noise, but Matthew bravely ignores this and begins to make his way down the spiral stairs. Halfway down, he whispers, "Jess, is that you?"

There is no response. He can hear rustling coming from the kitchen. Matthew starts to feel very afraid. He's struggling to regain control of his breathing and his thoughts. Surrounded by an eerie darkness, he stands barefoot on a single step in the middle of the staircase. The only slight shimmer of light is coming from the mirror at the bottom of the stairs. As the rustling noise continues, Matthew looks around for something he could use as weapon to defend himself. His eyes fall on the solid-gold picture frame on the entry table. Trying to make as little noise as possible, he slowly tiptoes down the stairs and picks it up. Now closer than ever, Matthew plucks up his courage.

"Jess, Eve, if it's any of you two in the kitchen, you need to answer me now," he says, his voice shaky.

Still nothing.

Closing his eyes, Matthew is about to charge his way in when he suddenly hears a humming, which instantly knocks him off track. Again, he says, "Jess?"

Practically shaking from head to toe, he slowly places one foot in front of the other, heading straight towards the kitchen.

"Last chance, Eve or Jess, this isn't funny."

Silence.

"Fine, have it your way. One, two, three."

On three, Matthew courageously charges towards the kitchen door. But as soon as his feet reach the doorway, a gust of wind blows so forcefully that it shoves him across the hallway. Falling onto his back as he lets go of the solid-gold picture frame. It flies across the floor and smashes to pieces. Matthew lands next to the bottom step. His heart feels as though it's going to burst at any moment. Looking up, he sees a grey mist drifting from the kitchen. The dark mist surrounds Matthew, who is stiff and locked with fear. As he takes in what is happening around him, his eyes protrude from their sockets. He no longer feels in control of his emotions or his movements.

Taking over the room, the mist begins to thicken. It encircles his body and the accompanying dark energy travels deep into his mind. Frozen, Matthew hears a symphony. This calming piece of music is attached to the mist, which is making its way through his eardrums and taking over his sight. Once this deceitful mist is satisfied with the invasion of this petrified soul, its sends for its owner to appear. Standing in the doorway,

She's back!

She's standing in the doorway, with her head down low, her jet-black hair hanging past her thighs. Her hair drips a thick black substance. Her whole body is grey and covered in deep wounds that ooze the same sinister black bloody substance, which slowly rolls down her body, landing on the floor. She peers through the gaps in her hair, her lips black with the grotesque slime.

Matthew is still frozen. The only thing he still has is his sight. But he can't close his eyes, so he's forced to watch the horrific events taking place. He wants to scream, to run and lock himself away, but Matthew, unfortunately, has no such privilege.

As the black, bloody substance lands on the floor, it slowly begins making its way towards him. Reaching his feet, this evil liquid takes over his once innocent skin tone.

"Ring a' Ring o' Roses – her soul is mine. Ring a' Ring o' Roses – she's been chosen for the dark side."

As the rhyme is sung, the evil entity lifts her head. Her eyes are the deepest blood red. She charges at Matthew, her grey sharp teeth launching towards him. The sickening black bloody substance gushes from her mouth as she throws herself into his mind.

Matthew screams and jumps up with fright, breathing heavily. He looks around and sees that he is back in his bed, soaking wet, and covered head to toe in sweat. In sheer panic mode, he reaches out and turns the lamp on at the side of his bed. Patting his body to ensure he's in one piece, Matthew slowly looks to the other side of the bed. She's there. Matthew sees Jess; she's sleeping peacefully next to him. Feeling a huge sense of relief, he throws himself back on to the pillow and tries to regain control of his breathing and heartrate.

Why does this keep happening? His curiosity gets the better of him and, as he grabs the phone from off the side table, he notices it's 5 a.m. Wanting answers, Matthew types an internet search: *Realistic paranormal nightmares what do these mean?* The fourth result grabs his attention. It says, "*Shadow Person – Wikipedia.*" Clicking the highlighted link, he's directed straight to the following explanation:

"A sleep paralysis sufferer may perceive a 'shadowy shape' approaching when they lie paralyzed and become alarmed.

"One subject says 'You don't see shadow dogs or shadow birds etc. You see shadow people. Standing in doorways, walking behind you, coming at you on the sidewalk.'"

Reading this, Matthew diagnoses himself. He is now *convinced* he's suffering from a sleeping disorder. Totally drained, he can't take another night of this insane, horrific ordeal. And so, he decides there's only one thing for it: he's going to the doctor in the morning. Putting his phone back on the side table, he lies facing Jess. Taking in her expression and features, he begins to smile. She's so beautiful. The locket around her neck hangs over her shoulder, glistening. He reaches out and tucks her hair behind her ear. Slowly, Jess begins to wake.

"Shh… Sorry, I didn't mean to wake you."

Opening her eyes, Jess pulls back as she takes in Matthew's appearance.

"Why are you soaking wet?"

"Shh, go back to sleep. It was just a bad dream, don't worry."

Climbing out of the bed, Matthew heads to the en-suite for a shower. Taking off his soaking wet pyjamas trousers and his boxer shorts, Matthew turns the shower on and climbs in. The bathroom fills up with steam. Matthew jumps as he turns around and sees Jess standing behind him. Their eyes lock. The hot water sprays them softly in the face and droplets fall from their lashes and roll down their features. As Jess's body brushes against Matthew's body, her skin becomes slippery with soap, like his. Jess reaches up and throws her arms around his neck, passionately kissing him. Her lips travel down his neck, then all the way to his lower abdomen. Unable to hold his voice in any longer, Matthew moans out loud with pleasure.

Her hands firmly grasp his thighs and Jess reaches for his hard, erect penis, placing him inside of her mouth. She sucks and allows it to travel to the back of her throat. Matthew groans louder and louder with ultimate pleasure.

He runs his fingers through her hair and grips it, tugging at the roots gently. Jess jumps up and without giving Matthew time to process her next move, she wraps her legs around his waist. Stumbling slightly as he takes her weight, he places one hand on the wall of the cubicle. Fully aroused, he becomes even harder. Kissing him passionately, Jess places her hand in the tight curls of Matthew's hair. Moaning out loud, she begins tugging hard at the roots and pulls his head back.

"I want you. Give yourself to me, now, Mr Honey," she whispers directly into his ear.

Breathing heavier and heavier, Matthew surrenders to his urge. Impassioned in the moment, he slides himself deep inside her. The pair begin moaning with gratification as they receive and feel one another. Unable to control his urges, his needs, his desires, he begins forcefully thrusting into Jess as her sexual groaning gets louder. Jess pulls his hair once more and says, "Give yourself to me."

He desperately tries to hold back, but he can't do it. As she's sucking and kissing him on the neck, travelling passionately to his lips, Matthew surrenders to her desires and sexual commands. Letting out one final moan, he thrusts her hard for the last time and whispers, "I'm coming."

Feeling his erect penis pulsate inside of her as he lets out his release gives Matthew an intense sense of euphoria. Breathing heavily, Jess drops her legs and Matthew groans as he leaves her body. Regaining his balance, as the cramp slowly eases he squirts soap on his hands and begins rubbing it all over Jess's body. They're both smiling. Kissing her once more on the neck, Matthew whispers into her ear, "I think I love you."

"I know."

Immediately regretting his words, Matthew blushes. He quickly washes the soap off his body and gets out the shower. In a panic he says, "I'm sorry, I don't know where that came from."

Wrapping the towel around his waist, he heads back into the bedroom.

Jess remains in the shower. Her eyes flame as his DNA travels around her internally. Feeling empowered, she smiles a deceitful smile as she plays with the locket around her neck.

CHAPTER TWELVE

Doctor, I Think I'm Going Insane

Matthew sits on the stiff, red leather, built-in couch in the waiting room at his local doctor's surgery. Much to his horror, he's surrounded by poorly patients big and small, who are continuingly coughing and sneezing. Trying to distract himself from the possible illnesses he might contract whilst waiting for the doctor to call his name, Matthew begins perusing the leaflets and general health advice neatly stapled on the walls. There is a detailed display about the possible effects of type two diabetes, with pictures showing general care tips. His attention is suddenly drawn to the small ocean-blue leaflet with tiny pastel multi-coloured fish around the border. He smiles at the title: "Little Fishes Parent and Toddler Group". His thoughts begin to drift back to a wonderful time in his life and a memory sacredly stored away surfaces.

Lauren is sat with Eve on her lap, with her usual radiant smile plastered across her beautiful face. She's clapping tiny Eve's hands together. The group are sat in a circle waiting for the song to start. The introductions begin and each child, along with their parent/parents pretends to be little fish while singing their names. Eve is giggling away and is becoming extremely hyperactive. She's watching her just as giddy daddy, who simply can't sit still and behave himself. While the introductions are being made, Matthew is wriggling around Lauren and Eve pretending to be a little shark. Singing along with Eve, he reaches over and grabs at her tummy as she sings her name. Lauren joins in the fun and attempts to save tiny Eve from the little daddy shark.

Matthew hears a sudden loud cough and feels a splutter down his neck, snapping him out of his happy memory and back into reality. He can't help but think once he leaves the building he's actually going to be physically ill, as well as mentally challenged. With his patience wearing thin, and his stomach turning at the thought of the germs resting on his neck, Matthew walks across the full waiting room to speak with the receptionist.

"Excuse me… Can you tell me how much longer the wait is, please? I've been sat here forty minutes already."

The receptionist peers over the frames of her glasses at Matthew, with a what-do-you-want-me-to-do-about-it expression on her face, she then looks back at the screen.

"Name?"

"Matthew Honey."

"You're next."

"That's great, thank you."

Squirting a generous amount of hand sanitizer onto the palms of his hands and wiping the excess onto his neck, Matthew makes his way back to the waiting room. This time, he decides to sit well away from the serial sneeze offender. Looking around, he sees people from all walks of life: little ones who just refuse to sit still, teenagers continually tapping away on their mobiles, and the rest either look exhausted or have a magazine or book in their hands, potentially to hide from the chaos of the waiting room. As Matthew looks up, something grabs his attention. He sees another informative billboard, this one aimed at mental health. No sooner has he started to read the advice than he hears, "Matthew Honey, please."

There he stands, at last. Mid-forties, with a full head of thick black hair, along with a few cheeky greys peeping through, the casual-looking doctor wears brown loafers and navy-blue cord pants, with a white and blue floral-patterned shirt, the top button loose. His energy seems relaxed and calming.

Relieved, Matthew looks to the doctor and impulsively says, "Thank God for that." Turning a slight shade of pink with embarrassment as everyone's eyes glare at him, he laughs nervously under his breath. He didn't mean to say the words out loud. He reaches out and shakes the doctor's hand. "Matthew Honey. Don't worry, doc, I'm not contagious, I'm just nuts," he says, once again without thinking.

Matthew lets go of the doctor's hand. He seems relieved and unsure whether to join in and laugh or call for security. "Not a problem. Mr Honey, would you like to follow me, please? We're in room four," the doctor politely responds.

They walk along the narrow airy corridor. The walls are pastel green and look like a coat of paint is long overdue. There are tiny chips and black marks, and you can see where children have run their mucky fingers across the wall. There are images of the most wonderful sights of English scenery hanging at eye level, as well as the occasional medical helpline poster. They arrive at room four. On the brown mahogany door is a beautiful gold plaque that reads, "Dr. Rushmore, GP, BMA".

"Please, after you."

"Thank you."

As they enter the room, which is extremely messy and totally unorganised, Matthew's OCD makes an appearance. There are heaps of paperwork sprawled out everywhere. Matthew struggles with a strong urge to put some order to the room. A white sheet has been rolled out across the medical bed in the corner of the small space and multiple items of medical equipment are lying around the room. The room has the same relaxed presentation as the doctor himself. Clearly, you don't receive cleaning and organisational lessons when you qualify to have letters placed after your name.

"Please, take a seat. I'm Dr Rushmore. How is it I can help you today?"

"Erm, well, I don't know where to start really. Honestly, between me and you, doc, I... well, I think I'm losing my mind." Placing his head in his hands he continues, "I'm convinced I'm losing it. Have you read through my notes?"

"Yes, I am aware of your situation and can I say, my condolences to you and your family for your loss. It can be hard for anyone to process, losing a loved one. I'm sure you're not losing your mind. Please explain. I'd like to understand what is making you feel this way."

Matthew's shoulders slump and he takes a deep breath in.

"Do you mind if I call you Matthew?" Dr Rushmore asks.

"No, it's fine, I prefer it."

"Thank you. Okay, Matthew, let me just say, whatever is said in this room, I want you to know it is completely confidential; please don't be nervous. My job is to help, not judge."

Biting the bullet, Matthew says, "Lauren, my deceased wife, well, as you'll have probably read, she's been gone for some time now."

"Yes."

"Well, doc, since then, I've not... how can I say this... Doc, what it is, erm, since Lauren, I haven't, you know, *been* with another woman."

"Okay." Dr Rushmore continues to make notes as Matthew speaks.

"Well, a few days ago, *unplanned* and completely randomly, I met a woman."

"Okay. I see. And how do you feel about that?"

"Well, that's just it, doc. I can't get my head around how I feel about it because ever since, I've been suffering with terrible nightmares."

"Okay. What is it you actually mean when you say nightmares: bad dreams, sleep walking, that sort of thing?"

"Oh no, doc, these nightmares scare the, pardon my language, shit outta me. And I'm a grown man. I wake up soaked from head to toe with sweat."

"Can you recall what any of these nightmares are about?"

"Yeah, doc, it haunts me, it's the same thing every night. The most horrific, demonic sort of woman appears. It feels real, it feels as though it's physically happening to me. I mean, look at my hand – right, so in one of the nightmares I had my chain with a cross on in my hand. The cross cut me. Doc, how's that happened? Look, you can see these cuts are on my hand, here, now, in real life. And, well, my daughter, Eve, she's changing too, doc. I don't know what's gotten into her, she seems distant. I just can't explain it. Everything's changed so much in such a short space of time, ever since I met Jess. I don't know, maybe it's too soon, maybe I should just stay alone." Matthew sighs with frustration and then continues, "You see, doc, this is what it's like, I'm driving myself insane. I feel mental. I'm constantly arguing with myself."

Dr Rushmore stops typing.

"Matthew, you shouldn't use the word mental when talking about yourself. I can see that you're not 'mental', as you put it. What you're experiencing is perfectly normal. The cuts, can I see them?"

Matthew passes his hand to Dr Rushmore. "Normal?"

"Do you have any idea how this may have happened?"

"Well, the chain I had in my hand, it's now snapped. It came off in the night."

"Matthew, there's really no need to panic. You must have been physically creating the movement whilst you were sleeping, and your mind has performed a reflection of the movement within your dream. Now, tell me, Matthew, would you say you think about Lauren at all during the day, or at night?"

"Dr Rushmore, I think about Lauren non-stop."

"I believe what you're experiencing is actually a step forward in the grieving process."

"Huh, a step forward…"

"Yes. You see, what you are doing, Matthew, is forcing guilt upon your mind; this is natural. You're thinking of moving on and contemplating creating a new family lifestyle for you and Eve, and as much as you want it, deep down somewhere, you don't believe you deserve it. You don't believe you deserve to receive this life, because your deceased wife, Lauren, doesn't have the same opportunity. It's perfectly normal. During the day your conscious mind is preoccupied and distracted by the day-to-day activities. It's a very different story during the night. Night time is when our unconscious mind takes the reins, so to speak. The unconscious mind is what we use to daydream. This is where our imagination is located. Currently yours is choosing to process guilt and portraying your worst fears at night. Would you say you struggle to drift off to sleep?"

"Doc, that makes so much sense, I think you're right. Erm, I actually haven't struggled to get to sleep. But, well, now I have a slight build-up of anxiety when it comes to going to sleep. It's draining me."

"Ah, I see. Okay, so we have two options, well, actually three options: you can wait and I will refer you to the sleep disorder clinic, I can prescribe you some sleeping tablets to try and help you relax, which will hopefully settle your unconscious mind, or we can send you away with nothing and I will monitor you, on an as-required basis. Which would you prefer?"

Matthew thinks about this for a second; he's not big on the whole taking medication hype, but nonetheless he gives in. He's so exhausted and truly can't function while sleep deprived.

"I'll take the tablets, please."

"Do you have any allergies to medication?"

"None that I know of."

The doctor types away. "Okay, so, Matthew, what I'm going to prescribe you is ten milligrams of temazepam for seven to ten days. You'll take one each night about an hour before you wish to go to sleep. They work extremely fast, so under no circumstances should you take them when driving, operating any heavy machinery or planning to cook a meal, and so on. The tablets can be addictive, so your course is seven to ten days *only*. I'm hoping this helps your mind learn to relax again, just whilst you're beginning to process living this new chapter of your life. Honestly, Matthew, it's quite normal. I'm not concerned, nor should you be."

"I know. I just suppose I never thought my life would come to this. I thought I would have my wife forever."

Dr Rushmore glances at the clock then hands Matthew the prescription. "Just so you know, the side effects are drowsiness, tiredness, nausea, anxiety and headaches. It's extremely rare, but if for any reason you experience severe changes to your body, such as blurred vision, irregular heartbeat, stomach cramps, or if the nightmares continue, stop taking the tablets immediately and come back to see me. It's all explained in the leaflet you'll receive. We're open Monday through to Saturday and I'm here every day. I'm going to book you an appointment for around ten days' time."

Matthew places the prescription in his pocket and shakes Dr Rushmore's hand. "Honestly, doc, thank you, I thought you were going to have me sectioned."

Dr Rushmore smiles. "Matthew, you're fine. It's a very traumatic experience, what you've had to cope with. Not only losing your wife, but becoming a single father is a big change. I'd expect you to go through these processes. After all, we're only human."

Leaving the surgery, Matthew's feeling slightly more at ease about his current situation.

Matthew pulls into the garage and sits alone with his thoughts for a moment, attempting to process the doctor's words and comprehend the reality of his current situation. He glances at the paper bag from the chemist resting on the seat next to him. Reaching across, he pulls the contents out of the bag. He reads the details on the box of medication and, upon seeing his name, Matthew suddenly feels an intense sense of inner sadness and devastation.

"So, this is what it's come to."

The surge of sadness is too much for him to bear. Dropping the bag on his lap, he cups his head with his hands and breaks down. He lets go of the internal strength he's built, he can't hold it in any longer. Gently sobbing, he sees images in his mind of his wife, his best friend, his Lauren. Being brave is a speciality of his, but the reality of starting this new chapter without her is beginning to process in his mind, and the pain, like a huge electric bolt of lightning, travels directly to his heart. He is apprehensive and unsure of what the right, or wrong, thing to do is. Regaining control of himself to a degree, Matthew wipes his face and checks in the rear-view mirror to ensure that his minor outburst isn't visible. He goes inside. The house is completely silent.

"Eve... Jess?" He gets no reply.

As he makes his way towards the kitchen, he looks at the entry table next to the door. Matthew shakes his head in disbelief, trying not to freak himself out. As the doctor's words circulate in his mind, he desperately attempts to reassure himself that it's all in his head.

"There's surely a logical explanation. It's fine. Don't freak out. Whatever you do, Matthew, just don't freak out."

The reality, unfortunately, is right before his eyes. The golden picture frame *has gone*. It's disappeared. Trying to soothe his mind and comfort himself, he begins speaking out loud: "It's okay, just keep breathing. It's all going to be okay."

Attempting to retrace his footsteps from this morning, he struggles. He was so embarrassed, in a rush to get out of the house after the words he so thoughtlessly blurted out to Jess, that he didn't even think to look at the table. Entering the kitchen, he quickly pours himself a glass of wine. Matthew doesn't acknowledge, or care, that it's only slightly past midday as he guzzles a mouthful. He urgently needs this cold alcoholic beverage. Regaining control of his thoughts, Matthew takes his phone out of his inside pocket and rings Eve. It goes to voicemail.

"Yeah, it's Eve, leave a message, or don't, not really bothered."

Beep.

"Eve, it's Dad. I've just got back to the house. Can you let me know where you are, please? I love you, darling."

Matthew hangs up and tries to ring Jess. But her phone also goes straight to voicemail.

"Your call has been forwarded. Please leave a message after the tone."

Beep.

"Hi, Jess, it's Matthew. Listen, I hope what I said this morning hasn't freaked you out. If it has, then I just want to say that I'm sorry. It's all new to me. Take care, special one."

He puts the phone back into his jacket pocket and grabs his wine, along with the bag containing the medication, and makes his way upstairs. As he stands in the doorway of his bedroom his mind decides to be unkind. No sooner has he placed one foot inside than he experiences a sudden and intense flashback from this morning's events. The steam circulating around them both, looking deep into her eyes, feeling the connection of bodily fluids as they intertwine with one another… Matthew hears the words he spoke: "I think I love you."

With a knot building in his stomach, and a wrench in his heart, Matthew shakes the image out of his sight. His face full of guilt, he breathes in deep. In one great big gulp, Matthew throws the wine to the back of his throat. Walking over to his bed, he places the bag from the chemist and the now empty wine glass on the bedside table. Sitting on the edge of the bed, he reaches for the silver cross and chain. As he's admiring the piece for its beauty and the memories it holds, Matthew slowly looks up. He smiles with his mouth but his eyes remain heavy as he desperately tries to regain control of not only himself, but his emotions. He embraces the moment, the peace, the tranquillity, the gentle vibrational energy as the memories flash in his mind. This stunning and pure piece of jewellery is more than just an object or a possession; it has meaning, it carries love.

As his attention drifts, suddenly it clicks: the *cameras*! Placing the cross on the side, Matthew rushes out of the room and makes his way to his home office. Unable to comprehend why he didn't think of this before, Matthew's practically running up the stairs to the second floor when he gets a strong sense that he's being followed. He isn't alone. The house is empty, and yet Matthew feels a huge presence behind him. Standing still, hearing the sound of his breath leaving his body, Matthew hesitantly says, "Eve?"

There is no response, and he shakes his head and continues with his mission, desperately attempting to ignore the anxiety building in his mind. But again, he can't help it. He feels as if someone's run up behind him and is now standing over his shoulder and staring intently at his face. He's too scared to turn around. Not only is his mind feeling this presence; his body feels it too as a huge gust of wind forcefully blows past him. It's freezing cold and carries a strong stench of death. He shudders. The hairs on his body stand to attention and the stench irritates his nostrils, travelling to the back of his throat and making him nauseous. The hallway becomes dark and remains cold and he can see the breath leaving his body. Matthew's eyes remain wide open and all his senses are heightened. Feeling as though he's being accompanied by entities unknown, and not the friendly kind, he slowly turns around… and sees there's no one there.

Slightly relieved at the confirmation that his imagination is once again running wild, Matthew lets out a big sigh. Not wanting to allow fear to take over, Matthew shrugs this off and heads to his office. But the eerie energy lingers, and he looks behind himself once more as he arrives at his office. There is nothing and no one.

Turning his attention back to the task at hand, he looks straight ahead and smiles. Proudly placed on the wall is the plaque Lauren made as a gentle reminder to them both of how it all began. When they originally decided to set up their own business and embark on this new adventure together, Lauren performed a grand unveiling of the plaque to mark this huge stepping stone in their life. There it is, shimmering away in all its glory, made with the brightest gold. It is the perfect addition to the mahogany door, along with the thoughtful personalised engraving on it:

Creation Station
The Honey Empire
♣♦M♦&♦L♦♣
Masterminds busy doing what they love

Matthew enters the office and sits at his desk. He puts his head in his hands, feeling exhausted, drained and confused. Even after Dr Rushmore's diagnosis, he's still saddened and unsure of the reasons why his mind is being so cruel. As he switches on the computer, his thoughts become overpowered by the unknown. He doesn't have any answers and he's apprehensive about the practicalities of looking for them. He's unsure about what he may see on the footage, but Matthew knows that the cameras never lie, and this scares him more than anything. As he's about to type in his password, suddenly his phone begins vibrating in his pocket. It's a call from an unknown number.

"Hello, Matthew Honey speaking."

"Hi, Mr Honey, how are you today sir?" says a voice with a slightly foreign accent.

"I'm fine, thank you. Sorry, I'm a little bit busy right now. Can I help you with anything at all?"

"Yes, certainly sir, I am Rahul calling in relation to your broadbanding there. Can I ask, Mr Honey, who is your current using provider?"

Matthew rolls his eyes. "Hi, Rahul, thanks for your call but I'm actually fine as I am. Thank you for checking, though."

"That is great news what I am hearing sir, but did you know that actually we are the cheapest in the world? You are being the lucky one today, Mr Honey. I would like to be helping you to be getting these savings of money, yeah."

"Look, I'm sorry, I don't want to waste your time…" But before he can finish speaking Rahul hangs up. "Hello… As if… Bloody cold callers."

He puts his phone on the side, and as he begins to type in his password it rings once again. This time it's not Rahul. Matthew sees "Hades Account" flashing. With an air of urgency, he stands up as he answers the call. "Hello, Matthew Honey speaking."

Matthew hears a familiar and somewhat eccentric voice at the other end of the phone. "Hi, Matthew, it's Bill, Bill Hades. I've been trying to get hold of you."

"Yeah, Bill, sorry about that, it's been hectic recently."

"So, I believe business is booming for both of us. Generate the wealth, ha-ha. Keep the pot growing, so to speak. These lavish luxuries and private jets won't buy themselves. Ha-ha, aye, Matty boy."

"Ha-ha, yeah, something like that, Bill."

"Look, I wanted to arrange a meeting with you. We're launching a new clothing brand globally and I need you to produce our adverts ASAP. I'm busy now but get that Danny of yours to call Vera and set up a meeting. I need this brand launching into the world urgently. As always, Matty, you're the man for the job."

"Yes, sure, don't worry, Bill. I'll get Daniel to set that up straightaway."

The call ends and Matthew, with a sudden burst of excitement, steps away from his desk and heads out of his office. His mind's swirling with elation, his sole focus the positive contribution life has just presented him with, and nothing more.

He makes his way back downstairs and enters the day room, stopping at the huge window and gazing out at the beauty of the beach. He's taking in the moment, embracing his success. Matthew feels amazing. Aware that the meeting needs to be set up immediately, he rings the head office.

"Good afternoon, Honey Productions, it's Daniel speaking."

"Daniel, it's Matthew."

"Hey Matthew, I've just got an email from Vera, you know, Bill Hades's PA. I was literally about to reply to her now."

"That's great. Daniel, do me a huge favour and fit them in as early as you can. I don't care if it's a weekday, or a weekend, this is urgent business. This job is massive, and you know what Bill's like, he wants everything three weeks ago."

"Yeah, of course, not to worry, I'll get to it, like, now. Oh, who's attending?"

"I presume the usual suspects, me, you, Christina, Bill and Vera. I think this one's tight knit, so unless we're told otherwise we'll keep it small."

"Okay, so you'd like me to liaise with Christina too, not a problemo, consider it done."

"Oh, don't forget to book the meeting room, and give the usual caterers a call once you've confirmed. Daniel, I'm counting on you, please do what you have to; just make this happen. The Hades Account is our biggest. And we've got the summer Honey P Party coming up, clay pigeon shooting and the ultimate barbeque. I promise to give you all extra clay to shoot at and prosecco on tap if we get this contract. How's that sound?"

Daniel needs no further encouragement. "I'm on it, best service, biggest smiles and exquisite food. Are you coming into the office today?"

"I've got a few things to sort out, so probably not. Any problems, just call me. Oh, and as soon as you've sorted the appointment, send an email, copying all attendees in, and put it in mine and Christina's diaries."

"Sure, will do."

"Thanks, Daniel."

"You're welcome, pleasure as always."

As they end the call, Matthew puts his phone back into his pocket and immediately performs a victory dance. The Hades Account is worth a fortune and is one of Honey Productions' main revenues of income.

Heading back into the kitchen on his new emotional high, Matthew pours himself a glass of wine; this time, it's in celebration. Looking to the floor, he shakes his head in complete astonishment. What is happening? How has his life become this whirlwind rollercoaster ride? Unsure of the answer, as he places the almost-empty bottle back in the fridge.

He heads back upstairs to return to his previous task. Still on a high, he pays no attention to the eerie energy still present in the house. As he enters the office, he sits at his desk and, without any interruptions this time, successfully logs on to the computer. Stopping for a brief moment, Matthew once again feels slightly apprehensive of what he might uncover. He rests his elbows on the desk and considers the fact that what he could uncover could bring him down off his high. He places his palms together and crosses his fingers, as if he is praying. His thoughts a whirlwind, Matthew tries to process the pros and cons of viewing the footage from last night. Matthew strongly believes that if he at least watches the footage, and indeed sees nothing, which after his visit with Dr Rushmore he's sure he won't, then he's certain he will no longer remain stuck questioning the unknown. Starting this new chapter is a huge step forward, and in order to complete this transition, he needs closure on the strange happenings of the night. With this his final thought, Matthew decides he's going to watch the footage.

Guiding the mouse, he clicks on the folder marked "CCTV Spy Cam". Instantly a split screen appears, but wait – it's black on both sides. It can't be. Matthew's confused. He searches every file on the computer to ensure it hasn't been recording in a different format, but has no luck. He is unable to locate the footage from the cameras. Even the live footage that should be filming now. Standing up, he heads out of the office. He makes his way over to the camera on the edge of the picture frame facing Eve's room and reaches up. Straightaway he sees the huge error he's made. In his impulsive decision to use the cameras, and rushing, not wanting to get caught out, he forgot one important thing. Matthew forgot to turn the camera on. Walking into his bedroom, he does the same check, and no surprise, once again he sees the camera isn't switched on. Feeling slightly insane, Matthew laughs to himself as he sits on his bed. Staring blankly, he's unsure of how to feel.

He opens the drawer on the bedside table and pulls out a strip of tiny keychain-sized pictures. As he's admiring the images he lies back on his pillow. The strip has multiple black and white photo-booth images on it showing a young Matthew and Lauren. These innocent images were taken the night he proposed to her. Lauren's proudly waving her hand in the air, showing off her ring, which cost Matthew a tiny expense of twenty English pounds. Lauren's unaware of the value and doesn't care. All you can see in these tiny images is the true love and happiness that has been captured. Tears once again form in Matthew's eyes as he relives the memory. As the teardrops fall, one after the other, onto the pillow, Matthew wipes his face. He places the strip back into the drawer, makes his way back into the office and switches off the computer. Grabbing his phone from his pocket, Matthew attempts to ring Eve.

"Yeah, it's Eve, leave a message, or don't, not really bothered."

Beep.

"Eve, it's Dad, call me when you get this, darling."

Suddenly, the front door bangs!

CHAPTER THIRTEEN

Let's Start Again…

Matthew rushes down the stairs to see Eve and Jess stood in the hallway surrounded by shopping bags. They both look extremely pleased with themselves. Slightly relieved, Matthew smiles as he makes his way over to Eve. Squeezing her tight and kissing her on the head, he instantly feels her happiness.

"Darling, I was getting worried, your phone kept going to voicemail."

"Sorry, Dad."

"It's okay, you're home now. Where've you both been?" Making his way over to Jess, he reaches out and gently kisses her on the cheek. "Hey, you."

"Hey, handsome."

"Oh my goodness, Dad – we've literally had the best time. Jess took me shopping and helped me pick out some new clothes. Then we had lunch and, oh, sorry, my battery died. I didn't take my charger."

"Evelyn Jade, I wish you'd change your voicemail message."

"Why, what's wrong with it?"

"Erm, yeah, it's Eve, leave a message or whatever, not bothered."

"Dad, what you see is what you get. I'm as blunt as they come." Laughing, she continues, "Plus it's the truth, I'm not bothered. You always told me never to lie. So technically it's your fault."

"It's always somehow my bloody fault." He gently shakes his head. "What have we got here, then? Looks like you two have been on a mission, wow."

"We really have had a lot of fun together, haven't we, Evelyn Jade?"

"The best."

"So, come on, then, show me what you've spent my money on."

"Oh no, Dad – Jess bought all this."

Mortified, Matthew says, "Wow, Jess, erm, thank you so much for the gesture, but please, how much do I owe you?"

"Don't be silly, Matthew, please, it's my treat."

Eve's smiling away. "Dad, let me show you what I've got."

Making her way into the day room, Eve starts pulling out items excitedly. Stopping in his tracks, Matthew turns to Jess and grabs hold of her hands. He looks deep into her eyes and says, "Thank you. Honestly, I haven't seen Eve this happy and chatty in a long time. Please let me take you and Eve out this evening, it's my treat. Actually, I'm not taking no for an answer."

"Thank you, Mr Honey – I mean, Matthew – that would be lovely."

As they enter the room Matthew and Jess can hear Eve wittering on to herself. She's pulling out all the items in the bags and placing them on the couch.

"Eek, I forgot I got that. Dad, you've got to see this dress that Jess picked out for me, it's ruby red."

"They're all amazing, darling. Listen, I've decided I'm taking us all out this evening. Maybe you can wear one of those beautiful dresses since I missed the ultimate changing room catwalk show, which of course I've become accustomed to."

Shoving the items back in the bag, she says, "This day's just getting better and better." Making her way over to her dad, she kisses him. "Oh, look, here's what we got for you."

Eve pulls out a solid gold picture frame and passes it to her dad. Beautifully positioned inside the frame is the picture which had gone missing from the entry table. Holding the frame in his hands, Matthew's unsure of what to say or do.

"Look, see, I put the picture in for you already."

"Darling, where's the old frame?"

"Well, I went to get breakfast this morning and the old one was broken on the kitchen side. The glass was shattered and everything." Holding her hands up in the air, she says, "I didn't do it. It was Jess who suggested we should get you a new one as a surprise."

He looks at the image inside of the frame, trying to digest Eve's words. Not wanting to look too shocked, he says, "Yeah, of course, that's great, thank you, darling."

With all her new possessions crumpled up and shoved back into the bags, Eve piles these up in her hands and begins making her way upstairs. Her energy is beaming brighter than the stars and she's full of life, practically skipping up the staircase. Smiling, Jess goes to follow, and as she reaches the door, Matthew holds her arm, gently stopping her in her tracks.

"Jess, can I have a word, please?"

"Yes, of course."

Looking out into the hallway, Matthew shuts the door. As he puts out his hand, he says, "Please, sit down."

Jess sits, looking slightly alarmed and confused by Matthew's actions.

"I wanted to say something about my choice of words last night."

"Oh, Matthew, honestly, it's fine. You really don't have to explain anything."

"No, I do. Really, I do." He takes a deep breath and prepares himself for the words he's about to say. "So, I haven't been myself recently. I truly thought I was getting to a point where I was rebuilding my life in all areas and, well… not fully, but slowly beginning to accept and move forward from the murder of my wife. Yet the more

I've thought about this being my reality, the worse my state of mind has become."

"Because of me?"

"Oh, good lord, no, not because of you. No, no, no, no, no. Please don't think that. It's not coming out right at all this. What I'm trying to say is, well… erm, since I met you I've not been sleeping too great. This isn't to do with you, honestly." Holding her hands, he continues, "Today I decided enough is enough and I went to see the doctor. I haven't been to the doctors for a long time. Do you remember last night when you asked me why I was soaked?"

"Yes."

"Recently, I've been experiencing bad dreams of sorts, but they feel real. The broken picture frame, well… I broke that last night while I was sleeping." He gently shakes his head as he knows this is making no sense and making him sound slightly insane. "Look, I don't want to go into too much detail, but I think I'm sleep walking. I'm hoping I've now found a solution, so I guess why I'm telling you this is because I'm truly surprised you've not run a mile. Both me and Eve haven't been the easiest to deal with. And I suppose I just want to thank you for your graciousness."

Throwing her arms around his neck, Jess gazes deep into his eyes. She climbs on top of his lap, leans over and whispers onto his lips, "All is forgiven, Mr Honey."

She kisses him passionately. They both become aroused as they receive one another's energy. Running her fingers through his hair and feeling him growing inside of his pants, Jess whispers into his ear, "*Mi temono.*"

Suddenly, Matthew feels an unknown energy radiating at a rapid rate throughout his body. His nerves are awakened by this mysterious and unexplainable tingling sensation. Feeling both pleasure and pain, Matthew is confused as he tries to accept this new-found orgasmic energy which is taking over his body. But it's hard. His natural urge is to fight against this, but his body, which is surrendering, won't allow his mind to take control. Powerless, Matthew begins moaning out loud as Jess tugs at his hair. Gradually giving in to this intense sense of euphoria, his eyes close.

As she sees and feels his submission, her eyes start to change. Her deep black pupils appear to have taken over. No white is visible. Her eyes are like gaping holes in her face. She's taking possession of Matthew's soul, bit by bit, and she's now absorbing him through the windows of her eyes.

An intense grey mist surfaces slowly from the darkest and deepest parts of her eyes. It takes the form of a cross, a cross that is upside down. As she feels Matthew submissively embracing her presence and becoming more aroused by the second, she reveals her true intention. Taking ultimate control of the moment, she unzips his pants and instantly places him securely inside of her. Grinding her body on top of his, she leans and bites his lips. Drawing his blood, she embeds her teeth deep inside of his skin. Clenching her legs tight, she begins sucking the DNA from Matthew's body. As his blood travels down her throat and as they become one, the orgasmic pleasure accelerates her into her true form. As Matthew's erect penis moves deeper and deeper inside of her, she commands, "*Aperto.*"

Matthew's eyes snap open. Suddenly his phone begins vibrating, breaking their connection. Matthew is somewhat confused, unaware of how they have ended up having intercourse. Jess climbs off him, and as his erect penis slides out of her body and lands on his trousers, he moans.

Jess whispers, "Next time."

Regaining control of his mind, Matthew coughs. He shakes his head, trying to work out what's just happened. As he pulls away from Jess, his phone once again begins vibrating and beeping loudly. Reaching into his pocket, he sees he has an email from Daniel, and the heading reads: "Appointment Confirmation – Hades Account."

Making her way out of the day room, Jess leaves a very flustered and confused Matthew behind. Trying to regain control of himself, he clicks on the email, which reads:

Sent: Daniel Thompson
To: Matthew Honey, Christina Hart, Bill Hades, Vera Jenson
Subject: Appointment Confirmation – Hades Account

Dear All,

Re: Appointment Confirmation – Hades Account

Further to my conversation today with Vera, I am pleased to confirm the following appointment has been booked:

Date: Sunday 7th July
Time: 14:30
Location: Honey Productions, Canterbury
Meeting Room 5

On arrival, please make your way to the reception area and ask for Daniel Thompson.

If you require any further assistance, or if for any reason you need to rearrange the appointment, please do not hesitate to contact me on either my direct dial or email.

With kindest regards,

Daniel Thompson
Receptionist
Honey Productions

Eve is wrapped up in her own delightful little world in her bedroom. Wearing a huge smile, she's unloading all her new items. Carefully taking each expensive designer piece of clothing out of the bags, she sets about placing the garments individually onto matching gold padded silk hangers. Oozing excitement, Eve can't wait to add her newest additions to her already amazing clothing collection. She makes her way over to her gorgeous uniquely crafted, built-in white wooden wardrobes on the far side of the room. She opens the double doors, revealing the wonderfully organised contents. All Eve's clothes are arranged not only by colour, but by season too. It's like a work of art. Admiring each individual piece as she places it in the correct order, Eve feels spoilt and completely fabulous.

Once her work of art is complete, and her new clothes have a confirmed spot in their new home, Eve grabs her diary and sits at her desk. The thick, red, leather-backed book, which is filled with all her deepest secrets and true thoughts, is her most sacred possession. Flicking through until she lands at an empty page, Eve grabs her blue-ink fountain pen and begins writing a new entry:

"Today I got my wish, today I got to spend the day with a woman!!! A woman who could very well be the figure I've been searching for. We went shopping, a real girl's day shopping, it has been amazing. I literally feel on top of the world."

Before Eve has time to finish her entry, a cold breeze blows through her room. Shivering, Eve feels the hairs on her body quickly standing to attention. The temperature is sub-zero and it carries with it a nauseating stench. As it hits the back of her throat, Eve begins to retch. All her senses are awakened by this overpowering, disturbing manifestation, which is developing at a rapid rate. Dropping her pen onto the page, Eve splashes ink across the paper. Suddenly she no longer feels alone. She feels someone breathing over her shoulder and blowing directly down her ear. Taking in a deep breath, she slowly turns… but no one is there.

Exhaling with relief, Eve gets up from her desk and walks into the en-suite. Switching the light on, she makes her way to the ceramic white sink. She turns on the taps and splashes the freezing cold water onto her face. With her head in her hands, Eve slowly begins to hear a symphony of humming. The water which is flowing freely from the tap and gathering in Eve's hands unexpectedly turns black. Jumping with fright as the black liquid takes over her once innocent skin tone, Eve hears the hummed tune being repeated over and over, getting louder and louder. Suddenly, the light begins to flicker on and off.

She stands completely stiff as her sense of fear takes over. Alongside the eerie and yet enchanting rhythm, Eve can hear the sound of each deep breath as it leaves her body. The light stays off, it feels as though the darkness she's surrounded by is her new light. Too frightened to speak, and aware of the unnatural energy radiating from behind her, Eve's unable to contemplate running out of the bathroom.

The bathroom suddenly fills with light. Eve looks up. Staring at her reflection, Eve sees that the mirror tells no lies. Behind her stands the most horrific and terrifying demonic grey woman. Her jet-black hair is hanging heavy on either side of her face, and black blood is seeping from the cracks around her mouth. Her whole body is oozing the same black substance. She's back! Eve's heart is racing. "Please stop it!" She shouts.

Suddenly, Eve manages to regain the use of her legs and run. Without looking back, she flings her bedroom door open and bursts out of her room on to the landing and bumps into her dad.

"Oh, you okay kidda?" Matthew says as he catches her.

"Yeah. Erm, sorry." Eve says in a fluster.

"Are you sure? You look like you've seen a ghost."

"Yeah – I'm fine Dad."

"Okay." Matthew replies with a smile.

Not looking back, Eve then rushes down the staircase.

CHAPTER FOURTEEN

Medication Time

Night has fallen. Just a few hours ago the village of Hythe was filled with laughter and life – now, the same pathways are silent and still. There is not a soul on the streets, not a seagull in the sky. No form of life can be seen. The lampposts are lined up symmetrically and one or two of the lamps are flickering. Grey waves begin mounting with each gust of wind that blows, becoming fiercer and stronger with every descent as they crash against the sand. The tide is right in, pushing closer to the man-made grey brick wall that stands solid and separates the beautiful English beach from the streets. The moon is out, beaming up high in the jet-black sky. This magnificent sphere is captivating, stealing all the attention, without a star in sight.

Inside the Honey residence, a dark energy is making its way around the silent building. The mood throughout is eerie and the sleeping inhabitants' body hairs stand to attention. Travelling at a rapid rate, this dark energy has made its way into Eve's room, once again making the temperature sub-zero in readiness for the arrival of the Dark Empress.

Eve becomes unsettled in her sleep. She mumbles, "Mum…" She gets tangled in the bedsheets as she pulls them up to her neck, trying desperately to shield herself from the freezing energy circulating her room, though she remains unaware of the unpleasant force that is gradually invading her space.

The walls of the room begin to vibrate slightly. As the dark energy grows in power, they begin to shake. The solid wooden bed also begins to tremble, and then to rock violently back and forth. Eve's body shakes in-sync with the aggressive vibration, as if she's having multiple seizures, one after the other.

The grey, deceitful mist once again appears and begins to take ownership of the room. The mist becomes thicker with each second that passes, forcing its way through the gaps around the door and trickling through the golden keyhole. Eve is powerless. She's unable to wake and remains trapped against her own will, a victim to her own mind, being thrown forcefully around the bed.

Suddenly the rocking stops and the bed, along with Eve, becomes still. The heavy curtains begin to slide open unaided. Peering through the glass of the window is a single black raven. The intimidating creature stands stiff, staring intently at Eve. It is almost as big as the window itself, and with eyes that are the deepest red, this creature is a true reflection of its proud owner. The raven abruptly begins pecking at the glass. The sound reaches sleeping Eve's ears and she becomes emotional at the disturbance. She cries out, "Mum!"

"It is time, my child. *Non temere di me*," says a dulcet, eerie female voice. Eve's expression changes at the sound of the voice. Scrunching her eyes, Eve appears to be in pain. Suddenly she gasps as she begins to fight for her breath and her hands go to her throat. Her body is now limp. The vibration once again takes over Eve's bed and forcibly shakes the frame. Her lifeless body is thrown aggressively from one side to the other. As the spoken words develop in her mind, the evil energy attached to the sound begins to take ownership of Eve's living cells. With the transition almost complete, her facial features spasm.

Eve now lies motionless, her hands no longer holding her throat. Her eyes are open and she foams at the mouth. An unearthly grey tinge begins to spread rapidly across her once pure skin. Eve is no longer Eve. Her features slowly begin to showcase the evil that has devoured her soul. A deep crack spontaneously appears through the centre of her face and rips its way through her grey, lifeless lips. Black blood oozes from the rip, slowly dripping down Eve's face and rolling under her chin. It travels like a magnet to the necklace and locket hanging around Eve's neck, embedding itself all over the precious piece of jewellery. It no longer glistens. Much like its owner, this object has been tainted by evil.

The mist, now thick, is continually spreading and the once light, airy and innocent room is riddled with an unknown entity strong enough to make your soul crawl deep inside you. Suddenly, the wicked and cruel form of a shadowy woman appears… she's back! And once again, she's right on time.

The evil dark spirit walks through the mahogany door and makes her way over to Eve. Her expression is soulless, her head bowed low. Her bone-straight, jet-black hair hangs on either side of her face, dripping with the same sinister black substance that trickles from the gaping wounds on her body. It has a nauseating stench of death attached to it. With her neglected, unloved grey face, she peers through the gap down the centre of her hair with eyes that are the deepest red, just like the eyes of the raven. She moves her head slightly and looks across at the window. The raven pecks on the glass more furiously than ever, flapping with frustration. With a sudden sharp movement, she twitches her head – instantly, the window opens and the huge black bird glides into the room. Flapping her wings, the creature positions herself on the headboard of the bed. The intimidating and deceitful bird stands strong and proud, observing Eve's acceptance of the carefully calculated possession as the Dark Empress sings the words of the rhyme:

"Ring a' Ring o' Roses – your soul is mine. Ring a' Ring o' Roses – you've been chosen for the dark side."

As the final word is spoken, Eve's body shoots up and sits forward. Her eyes are deep black, like gaping bottomless holes in her face; not a glow or a shade of white can be seen. Deep cracks begin to form all over Eve's face and body, and sinister black blood oozes from each one. Her non-human form, her new identity, is gruesome. Eve is definitely no longer Eve. The raven flaps her strong black glossy wings and deep red blood flows from the gaps around her tiny eye sockets. The bird, much like her creator, is gaining energy and pleasure at the ownership of its newest member. The chosen one has finally accepted her fate. The wait is over.

The Dark Empress slowly moves closer to Eve's bed as she continues to sing her possessive rhyme with her deep dulcet tone:

"Ring a' Ring o' Roses – your soul is mine. Ring a' Ring o' Roses – you've been chosen for the dark side."

The Dark Empress reaches out. Her demonic, impure grey hand hovers over Eve's face. She is ensuring the possession of this young girl's mind, body and soul. Every cell is captured and controlled as the dark energy travels through her DNA, taking over its purity. She lays a cold finger on one of the wounds on Eve's face and collects some of the black substance. Bringing her finger to her mouth, she begins ingesting the sinful element.

"Soon you will shine, my child. The timing is almost right. We will finally be one, we will finally live our purpose. We, together, will unite and using the vulnerable, the impure, and the weak, we will build our empire. And the world will pay, as the universe becomes ours. *Non temere di me.*"

A look of deep satisfaction appears on the Dark Empress's face. She raises both her arms over her head with euphoria, embracing the moment. With her head held high, she opens her mouth, revealing her grey stained teeth. Black gushes from her mouth, dripping off each razor-sharp tooth. It flows down her chin as she squeals with ecstasy at her victory. She spits the black liquid across the room.

Her prized possession, Eve, has now become her mirror image. She appears impure but empowered by the events that are taking place.

The raven abruptly flaps up to the ceiling and, as she comes back down, she lands on Eve's shoulder. The blood from the Raven's eyes trickle down her feathers. The dark creature focuses her sight on Eve and shows her acceptance by pecking at the black blood on Eve's face. Receiving her energy, the intimidating creature squawks loudly.

Standing at the side of the bedframe, the Dark Empress wants to share the acceptance of this soul. Leaning forward, she uses her black, coarse tongue to lick the same wounds. Satisfied with the taste of the sinister substance, she begins to drink it. She extracts the liquid from Eve's body, gaining strength with every drop. Sat in the bed accepting her fate, Eve embraces each soul-draining draw as the blood departs from her body. There is no emotion upon her face and her voice is deep and no longer sounds her own as she says, "I'm ready… Mum…"

Just then there is a creak outside the room, startling the Dark Empress and her evil accomplice.

Matthew stands half naked in the hallway, wearing only his black pyjama bottoms. He is still a big groggy from the sleeping tablets he took earlier. He shivers as a draft of cold air flows over his body. His skin develops goose bumps and the hairs on his arms begin standing to attention. He notices what looks like smoke seeping from the cracks surrounding Eve's bedroom door. It slowly disappears into the darkness of the hallway. Staring attentively, and trying desperately not to freak out, Matthew slowly places one foot in front of the other and, with an air of caution, he makes his way over to the room. He feels each pump as his heart fiercely pounds against his chest, and the only sound he hears is the sound of his breath as it leaves his body. Tiny beads of sweat form on his forehead and roll down his skin. The hallway is dark and gloomy, and Matthew doesn't at all feel alone. His anxiety is heightened and he is no longer in control of his thoughts. Playing cruel tricks, his mind continues to send off signals telling him that someone is standing right behind him. But when he turns, he sees no one.

"Is anyone there?" he shouts out.

There is no response. The picture frames on the walls cast sinister shadows. The fear of the unknown has made the hallway appear haunting and long. He doesn't want to enter the room, but he knows he has to. His daughter could be in danger. Matthew gathers his strength, breathes in deep and grabs the doorknob… then jumps back. His mind is racing. The smoke continues to surround him, and now he can only just make out the door. He approaches it for the second time. He closes his eyes tight, grabs the doorknob and, as he breathes out, this time he courageously thrusts it open. Bursting into the room he shouts, "Eve!"

The room is freezing cold and dark. There is no sign of the strange smoke in the room. It's as if it never existed. Matthew's senses are on high alert. A sudden movement catches his attention. Eve's curtains are rippling and the window is open. Heading to the huge window, he battles against the wind as he shuts it tight. Shivering, he makes his way to Eve. Sleeping peacefully, she looks innocent, pure and beautiful. A mirror image of her mum. He smiles, leaning down to kiss his daughter on the head. He places his cheek onto hers and gently kisses her soft, warm skin. Feeling a sense of relief, he gradually moves away.

Eve suddenly mumbles, "Mum."

Smiling with sadness in his eyes, but feeling content with his observations, Matthew convinces himself that it's all in his head. He must be experiencing a side-effect from the medication he has taken. Still mumbling, Eve turns on to her side. As soon as she moves, Matthew' notices a black smudge the size of a fifty pence piece on her pillowcase. He reaches over and touches it, and the liquid attaches to his skin like glue. The thick, sticky liquid is freezing cold. Attempting to work out what it is, Matthew reaches his finger up to his nose and sniffs it.

"Eww."

His nostrils are instantly awoken by a pungent stench and a strong metallic taste forms at the back of his throat. Retching quietly so he doesn't wake Eve, he grabs the hand sanitizer and a tissue from the bedside table. He squirts the sterile liquid onto the tissue and tries to remove the unknown substance from his stained skin.

"Come off, damn it. For fuck's sake, what on God's green earth are you?"

The more he rubs, the deeper the liquid embeds on his skin. Matthew glances to the floor next to his bare feet and notices a similar-looking drop near the bed. He sees another, and another, and another. No sooner has he spotted these disturbing-looking black marks than they begin to disappear. Vibrating slightly, the floor absorbs each droplet.

Matthew is fully focused on working out what the substance is when suddenly there is a huge bang and a loud squawking noise. He jumps with fright. The sounds are coming from the direction of the window. Matthew looks up; there's nothing and no one there. But the window is once again open.

"What the f…" Desperately trying to not to freak out and wake Eve, Matthew gives himself a quiet pep talk. "Just keep breathing, it's probably nothing. I just didn't lock it properly. Yep, that's it, I didn't lock it properly."

Taking deep breaths in, Matthew bravely places one foot in front of the other and makes his way to the window. His adrenaline is kicking in and the combination of this with the cold sea breeze rapidly hitting his body sets him shivering, "Fuck me, that's cold."

Peering around the curtain, he observes the biggest, blackest raven he has ever seen, positioned on the lamppost below. He looks on in disbelief. The eyes of the huge bird are horrific; they stand out like red flames. No sooner has he locked eyes on this intimidating bird than she begins flapping her strong glossy wings with force. Matthew drops down to take cover. The huge raven rapidly ascends up to Eve's window, almost hitting him. He stumbles back slightly. As he stands, he sees the black bird has mysteriously disappeared.

Slamming the window shut and pulling the curtains tightly together, Matthew turns and sees Eve shivering in her sleep. Making his way to her, he pulls the loose bedsheets over her body.

"You're so beautiful, just like your mother, Evelyn Jade Honey."

As he moves Eve's hair out of her face, tucking it behind her ears, he becomes confused. Much like the black stains he saw on the floor, the black stain on Eve's pillowcase has also gone! Gently, he removes the pillow from off the bed without disturbing Eve and begins searching the fabric, front to back. Still he sees nothing. Looking to his hand, he sees the black stain has gone. Convincing himself it's definitely a side effect of the pills, and that actually it's not a big deal at all, he reaches for the hand sanitizer. This time Matthew coats all the skin on his hands.

He leans over Eve once more and picks up Gregg, placing the scruffy-looking bear next to her face. Looking above her bed, he stares at the heart-shaped, colourful collage of pictures. The beautiful shrine of the family he once had. As Matthew leaves the room, he reaches for the door and begins to pull it shut. Unsure and cautious, he changes his mind and decides it's best to leave the door open.

When he gets back to his room, Matthew sees Jess tucked up in bed asleep. Heading straight to the sink in the en-suite, he turns the cold tap on and repeatedly splashes ice-cold water onto his face. Catching his breath, he grabs the hand towel from the side of the sink and gently pats the water off his face. He breathes deeply and gathers his thoughts. As he lifts his head, suddenly the bathroom light flashes on and off. Matthew freezes. In his reflection, he sees, standing right behind him, the demonic woman. She's back!

With her head low, she twitches her body and, as her face spasms, Matthew sees her horrific features. She has evil red eyes that hold secrets you'd never want to know. Black, thick tears roll down her face. Staring in complete shock, Matthew is frozen.

She separates her lips and the black liquid begins gushing out of her mouth as she says in her deep, dulcet voice, "Let's play a game... It's time, you will see; she is mine."

Not wanting to accept this vision, Matthew blinks so harshly his eyelids feel as though they're about to bleed. Opening his eyes, he sees she's gone. He once again bends to the sink and cups the freezing cold water, rapidly throwing it in his face. It's so cold it takes his breath away. He gasps and lifts his head. His nerves are shattered. Looking down at his hands, he sees they're shaking uncontrollably.

As he walks back into the room, he sees a sudden movement from the corner of his eye. It's Jess. She's sat upright in bed. Mentally unprepared for this sight, Matthew jumps and practically throws himself across the bedroom.

"My God! Jess – you gave me a fright."

"Is everything okay? You seem on edge."

"Yes, I'm fine – just a bad dream."

He holds his chest to help regulate his breathing and slow down his heartrate. Feeling a bit calmer, Matthew goes to the bedside cabinet and grabs the packet containing the pills Dr Rushmore prescribed him. He unfolds the tiny leaflet which was inside the box. Scanning through it, he says quietly to himself, "No, not that, where is it – I swear these pills must cause some sort of hallucinations that he forgot to tell me about." Rustling the paper in his hand, he quickly becomes agitated. "Where is it?"

"Matthew – what is it you are looking for?"

"I knew I should have listened to my instincts. I don't take pills."

"Matthew, what's wrong?"

"Bloody hell… These pills."

"The pills to help you sleep?"

"Yes, the doc said they'd help to keep me asleep."

"Look, calm down, pass it here."

"Jess, you know I said I've been sleep walking?"

"Yes, I remember."

"Well, recently… erm, I'm not too sure how to word this, but I've not just been sleep walking."

"Okay."

"I've also, well… been seeing, things."

"Seeing things… What do you mean? Like what?"

"I can't explain it. The doc says it's normal, when moving on emotionally."

"Moving on, with me?"

"Well, yes, but I don't know, maybe it's too soon."

"It's never too soon to try anything. Tell me, I'm intrigued. What is it that has you wound up so tightly?"

"Never mind – please, just forget I said anything."

"Try me, or I could help you release some of that tension." Whispering, she continues, "Inside of me."

Really not wanting to go into detail, Matthew takes the leaflet out of her hand and places it back on to the bedside table. As he lays his head on the pillow next to Jess, he says nothing and gazes at her beauty. Looking deep into his eyes, Jess seductively tucks her hair behind her ear. The chemistry between them is extremely strong. Their energies are intertwined, calling for their bodies to become one. Moving closer to her, Matthew makes his move and leans in. They engage in a lengthy passionate kiss.

Holding Jess's head in his hand, he tugs at her hair with his firm grip as she begins moaning under her breath. Slowly he places one leg over her slender body and gets on top of her. Wearing nothing but her black-lace underwear, she embraces Matthew's toned physique as he places all his weight on her.

Running her hands round his back and holding him tightly in her arms, she digs her fingernails into his skin. Captured in the moment for its purity, he kisses her gently on the neck and gradually makes his way down to her chest. Jess moans louder. Placing her hands on his head, she grips his hair.

With his face at her lower abdomen, Matthew gently tickles her skin as he kisses his way down. Tugging at the lace French knickers she's wearing, he begins to pull them down. Jess lets go of his hair and places her hands behind her head, grabbing the sheets as she starts to gyrate her body on the mattress. Looking up, Matthew sees the enjoyment on her face. He removes the lacy underwear and kisses her there. Unable to contain herself any longer Jess shouts, "Matthew, I want you inside me!"

Immediately responding to this command, he licks her as she becomes wet with pleasure. Removing his boxer shorts, he places himself deep inside her. "Oh, Jess, you feel so good."

"Give yourself to me, Matthew."

Receiving every inch of him inside of her, Jess wraps her legs around his body tight. As he thrusts, she's holding him deep, passionately kissing him. Looking deep into his eyes, she's captivating his soul. Matthew's breathing rate has unexplainably changed and is now heavy. She rolls him onto his back. Maintaining eye contact, she kisses him one last time. As Jess begins moving up and down on Matthew, he moans with great satisfaction at the intense amount of pleasure he's feeling. "Oh, Jess, you're so tight."

"Give yourself to me, Matthew, I want you to let go inside of me. I want you to leave yourself inside of my body."

As she gyrates faster and faster on Matthew's hard erect penis, he surrenders. The build-up has become too intense. He moans once more and, grabs her hips and pushes Jess's body down, holding her still as he lets go of his semen and releases himself deep inside of her.

Matthew, still feeling the after effects of his orgasm, lies back embracing the body-tingling pleasure. Still on top of him, Jess leans down and whispers directly into Matthew's ear, "Your soul is mine."

As the words circulate around his mind, his eyes transform, turning a deep grey. Looking deep into the windows of his soul, Jess is taking over his sight, his mind and his existence.

Matthew pulls himself up. Jess, now sat on his lap, sees his eyes have turned black. The transformation is almost complete. "Welcome to the dark side," she says.

Matthew's mind begins to spin at a rapid rate. "Why?" he asks breathlessly.

"I am Jezebel, and she was never yours to keep!"

Matthew sees a flash image of the demonic empress; with this, his final vision, he passes out cold on the bed.

CHAPTER FIFTEEN

Defy the Odds: 7/7 at 7

"How long's left until they arrive?" Matthew asks.

"Erm, I think we've got around an hour or so," Daniel replies.

"When's Christina getting here? We need an urgent prep meeting."

"Erm, not sure, Matthew, shall I give her a call?"

"Yes please, and have you called the caterers?"

"Yep, they should be arriving any minute now."

"Well, they ain't here, so call them again!"

Matthew is a bag of nerves. He worries that he won't be able to concentrate as the recent terrifying delusional events continue to play on a loop in his mind. He is standing next to Daniel in the immaculate, glass-paned boardroom, waiting in anticipation for the arrival of Bill Hades. Glistening spotlights are beaming bright on the ceiling, creating a warming glow throughout the room. Ten high-back, red leather chairs stand alongside a huge glass table in the middle of the room. Sitting in the centre is a modern crystal-clear art deco vase, filled with ten of the whitest lilies.

Across the way on an oversized white wooden cabinet is a huge seventy-two-inch television. On the other side of the room sits another matching cabinet which contains a hidden built-in mini fridge. On top of the cabinet laid out in an organised fashion are ten Honey Productions personalised pens, pencils and notepads, matching the number of chairs around the table. On the edge of the cabinet, perfectly parallel and turned upside down, are ten stunning expensive crystal tumblers, along with the boardroom phone. Every item is positioned with precision. This organised and stunning room is immaculate; not a fragment of dust can be seen, nor a smudge on any of the glass.

Daniel places everything that's required out onto the table in readiness for today's meeting. Matthew, still on edge, jumps as the boardroom phone begins ringing.

"Hello, Daniel speaking. Oh, that's great. Yeah, sure, tell them I'm coming downstairs to meet them now. Yep. Okay. Thanks Kirsty."

"Who's here? It can't be them, I've not met with Christina yet."

"You've not met with who yet? What are you getting in a tizzy about?" Christina says as she enters the boardroom.

"Christina, thank God for that. What time do you call this?"

"Erm, plenty of time before the meeting is what I call this."

"That was the caterers by the way, they're in reception. I'll leave you both to have your prep meeting. Be back shortly." As he leaves the boardroom, Daniel whispers to Christina, "Good luck, he's been a right stress head all morning, not sure what's gotten into him."

Matthew waits for Daniel to go out of sight then sits at the table and places his head into his hands.

"Matthew, what's wrong?"

His appearance is slumped as he's looking at the floor.

"Matthew, please, talk to me. What's got you so wound up, is Eve okay?" Making her way across the room, she sits beside him. "Matthew – please, I beg you, speak to me, I'm getting worried. I haven't seen you like this since, well, since Lauren died. Is Eve okay?"

"Yeah, Eve's fine."

Shaking his head, Matthew quickly wipes away the single tear that rolls down his cheek.

Christina reaches out and holds him tight. "I miss her every day, too," she says gently. "I really do. She was the only best friend I had for all my life." Pulling back and holding onto his shoulders, she continues, "But Matthew, it's time. You can move on. No one will judge you and I'm sure Lauren would want you to be happy. Please, stop doing this to yourself; no matter how much we would love to have her here again, it's not going to happen. Lauren isn't coming back."

Matthew wipes his face and clears his throat. "I know. I'm sorry. I'm just tired. I haven't been sleeping too great recently, and it's draining me. My memory's going, my nerves are shot, and I'm being told by the doc that it's normal. It doesn't feel very normal, Chris."

"I know. Listen, we all know your heart will always lie with Lauren. She was amazing, she truly was. But look at what you actually have present in your life now. Eve seems to like this Jess, which is your biggest challenge of all. She has been raving to Melissa about her. The best advice I can give you is to just relax and stop being so hard on yourself. Enjoy this for whatever it is. No one is saying go away, have babies, get married and buy a house—"

"Don't even joke about that," Matthew interrupts.

"Matthew – look, stop being so serious, it's not what we're all saying. Life goes on; it's a fact. How do you think my mum and dad felt? They buried their child, the other half of me, my twin… it has been so hard on everyone, and we all just want you to be YOU again. Maybe without this Jess, or with her, but whatever it is, you must decide fast or you're going to make yourself ill. You look exhausted."

"I haven't slept. I can't sleep. I keep seeing this woman. I can't explain it because I can't remember all the details, but she's just constantly taunting me at night. I know it sounds mental, but I'm telling you this because, well, what have I got to lose, really? Nothing."

"Thank you."

"Thank you for what?"

"For speaking to me. I know how hard this is for you. Matthew, it's such a traumatic thing we've all experienced, you and Eve more than most. The reality is, your mind is clearly playing cruel tricks on you. I promise. Maybe you should head back to the doctor's after the meeting today."

"Can't. I've got to go straight home from here, there's something I need to check back at the house. Hopefully I'll get some closure. I promise, if it carries on, I'll go back. I think I'm just going to cool it off with Jess for a while. Stay friends. I only hope Eve doesn't freak out."

"I'm sure she'll understand. Now, off to the toilet and sort yourself out before Daniel comes back and Bill and Vera get here."

"Thanks, Chris, I'm lucky I have you." Matthew heads to the door and, as he opens it, he turns and says, "You truly are like her in every way, you know. Like you say, the other half."

Matthew walks into the toilets and heads straight for the sink. He turns on the taps and repeatedly splashes cold water onto his face. Water drips from his features as he keeps his head down, his arms spread out on either side of the sink. Matthew is desperate to return back to normal. Wiping the excess water from his face and straightening his tie, his mind unexpectedly throws him back into a happier time of his life.

Tiny Eve is toddling around their favourite clothes shop. She's pulling at her mum's arm, rushing to the tie rack. Lauren's smiling, Eve's giggling and Matthew's not too far behind them both. Gripping the ruby-red silk tie with her hands, she rips it from the tie rack. Eve mischievously runs off to her daddy and passes it to him, saying, "Daddy's tie."

Matthew snaps back to reality. He's wearing the ruby-red tie from his vision. As he takes a deep breath in, suddenly the light in the toilets flashes off and quickly flashes back on again. No sooner has he regained his sight, he's frozen stiff. She's standing right behind him. The Dark Empress has returned. As she lifts her head, black blood gushes out of her mouth. The light once again flickers off, and this time, when it comes back on, she's gone! Breaking down, Matthew sobs into his hands. "Please, just stop. Leave me alone. I can't take this any longer. Lauren, if it's you, I'm sorry! Please, I'm sorry."

Matthew's had enough. He curls up into a ball on the floor of the toilet. He can't cope with the mental torture. Physically and mentally drained, Matthew begins to cry uncontrollably.

Eve is backstage getting ready for her final ever production at the school theatre. She's been nervously practising all morning with her fellow musicians. Students of all ages, from all school years are congregated in the designated practice areas, excitedly preparing for the performance. This year, Eve has her very own solo and she's reviewing her notes, alone, in the corner of the dressing room. Once she's satisfied with her understanding of the chosen piece, her mind begins to wander. She's confused by the thoughts racing around her head. All the other girls, grouped together, are extremely giddy. They're all loudly giggling and chatting away to each other in the middle of the dressing room.

"That was the best we've ever done it. Girls, we're going to rock this."

"I know, I'm emosh, this is our last ever show. I'm gonna miss spending this time with you ladies. Group hug?"

"Group hug."

"Eve… Come on. Eve… Eve, are you ok?" says one of the girls, whose name is Emma.

"Huh? Oh yeah, I'm fine. Sorry, what were you saying?" Eve replies.

"Georgina was saying we're going to rock this. Group hug, come on, get in," Emma says.

"No, I'm all right, thanks, I'll stay here," Eve says.

Emma makes her way over to Eve, looking concerned. "Are you sure you're alright? You've been on another planet all morning?"

"Yeah, sorry, just thinking."

"About what?"

"Nothing, really."

"Well, I don't think it's quite nothing, you've barely spoken to any of us all morning. Eve, I know we haven't been close for some time now, and God only knows I've tried to be there for you, but you won't let me in. Please, don't do this, you're not alone. Speak to me."

"Emma, you won't understand, and I can't explain it anyway."

"Try me."

"Okay then, but you're gonna freak out."

"Like I said, try me."

"Something's coming," Eve states.

"Huh, what's coming?"

"Argh, see, it's hard to explain."

"Well at least try."

"The voices inside my head. Emma, they keep rambling on about my purpose."

"Voices?"

"Yeah, voices."

"So, I still don't understand, what's coming? Your purpose? I'm confused, what does that even mean?"

"I'm not sure. Look, come over here."

Grabbing Emma by the arm, Eve drags her over to the clothing rail where all their wonderful costumes hang in size order. She pulls Emma in between the items. She doesn't want anyone to see them or hear what she's about to say.

"This should be safe. Okay, be quiet and don't tell anyone."

"I won't."

"Emma, promise me?"

"I promise. Eve, you're scaring me slightly."

"Emma, it's serious. I keep hearing this voice. It's constantly whispering to me, telling me that my time has come, and saying that my purpose is greater than this, greater than me."

"Okay, that's a bit strange. Eve, I think that maybe you should go and speak to someone."

"I can't, Emma, I must trust the process."

"Trust the process? Eve, what on earth has gotten into you? Listening to these voices and letting them in? I mean, come on, that's not exactly normal, you must see that."

"Define normal, Emma?"

"Not that."

"You don't understand. I get it, it's fine, you're a clone and you'll always be a clone. Go on, off you go, get back to your group hug."

"Don't be mean, Eve. Why do you have to push people away all the time?"

"Push people away? Why, how close have you all been for me to push you away? I think you'll find you've stayed well away from me for a long time."

"No, I haven't! You wouldn't let me near to help."

"That's a load of crap and you know it. You dropped me at my time of need. My mum died, and we'd been friends since nursery. Ten years of friendship, for what? My mum made you tea and looked after you when you came and stayed over at our house, then you drop me when I need you most."

"Eve, I tried to help you. I can't believe you think that. You turned so nasty. What was I supposed to do? Allow you to keep having a pop at me cause my mum and dad are still alive and together? You made our friendship impossible."

"Impossible? Ha-ha, don't make me laugh. Shows your commitment to our long-standing friendship."

"Whatever, Eve. Seriously, don't ruin this for us; we've all worked hard for this and it's our last one. Just because you're unhappy doesn't mean the rest of us should have to change and tip-toe around you."

"Unhappy? You lot don't understand the meaning of the word unhappy, with your protected lives. You'll soon see. I can't wait for my day. You'll all see. It's not far away and then, well, I don't need to say what's going to happen next. I'll show you all."

"Whatever, Eve, I'm done trying to make you feel okay. Enjoy your misery."

"Yeah, enjoy your fake friendships. Pfttt…"

Separating the clothing and stepping back out into the dressing room, Emma goes off to join the group of girls, leaving Eve on her own.

Eve hears one of the girls ask, "What's up with happy over there?"

"Oh, the usual: everything's got to be about Eve. I give up trying," Emma replies.

"I don't even know why you try. I wouldn't give her the time of day after the way she treated you. Emma, you're better off with us anyway."

"Thanks, Georgie. I love you."

"I love you too, my beaut. Now, everyone, let's do this."

Eve comes out from the clothing rail and watches as Emma and her friends mischievously creep around backstage. Peeping through the huge, heavy red-velvet curtains, they're all getting excited as some of their parents are beginning to take their seats. Eve has reserved two seats on the front row. One for her dad, and the other for Jess. As the girls move on, Eve makes her way over and peers through the curtains. Neither her dad nor Jess are sat in their seats. The production is starting in less than thirty minutes, and as she's left her phone at home she can't call either of them to confirm if they're coming or not. She doesn't hold out much hope.

"Eve, come on, quick."

"Huh?" Eve turns to see Layla, a pretty red-headed girl from Eve's music class.

"You're spacing out again. Mrs Maztalerz is looking for us."

Layla pulls Eve along and they rush into the dressing room and grab their instruments. They are greeted there by their teacher, Mrs Maztalerz, a beautiful, fun and unique woman.

As Eve stands in the packed-out dressing room, her mind begins to drift again, this time to a happier time in her life. Hearing her teacher's voice, Eve snaps back to reality.

"Right everyone, settle down, settle down. Can everyone hear me? Hello?" *Cough, cough.* "Everyone! That's better. Okay, thank you. So does everyone have their instruments?"

"Yes, Mrs Maztalerz," the whole group of students say in sync.

"Okay, the parents are now arriving and we're about to start at any minute, so I want you all to get in your outfits. Introduction team, where are you?"

The group of twenty students put up their hands, Eve included.

"Can you all quickly get changed and line up over by the curtains on the correct side to which you are to be seated. And please, be quick, you're our opening act."

The curtains are closed. The conductor has just taken his bow, and he is now standing at the front of the stage with his back to the crowd. As the final parents take their seats, the curtains open. Sitting in her starting position, Eve looks anxiously to the front row. The seat she has reserved for her dad is, as predicated, empty. Disappointment and anger build up inside of her. She looks to the other seat and, astounded, she sees Jess. She's smiling, with her head held high. Their eyes lock.

Tapping his baton on the edge of the wooden stand, the conductor begins the musical performance.

The audience clap and cheer with pride at all the amazing pieces of music they are blessed to hear from their talented children. Performance after performance after performance. Before she knows it, it's time. Eve's moment has arrived. Mrs Maztalerz proudly makes her way to the front of the stage.

"How great have they all been? I'm blown away and so very proud of them all. Now, as many of you know, this is the last production for most of the students here as they leave school in a couple of weeks and will start the newest chapter of their lives. Many of them have bravely elected to perform a solo for you this afternoon, and so it is my greatest pleasure to introduce to you, on piano, the amazing, multi-talented Evelyn Jade Honey. Please, put your hands together as we welcome her to the stage."

Walking out nervously, Eve once again looks to the front row. She's so angry. Her dad still isn't sat in his seat. *He hasn't bothered to turn up, even though he knows how important this is!* The voice in her mind whispers the same words over and over on a loop. Standing alone, she looks to Jess and bows. She sits on the stool at the huge black grand piano. No sooner have her fingers graced the keys than her thoughts are taken over. She's given into the whispering voice and the last pure molecule of her soul has surrendered. With this final submission, her eyes become overcast and grey. She feels as though she's about to throw up, and her head begins to spin uncontrollably.

Under her breath, Jess whispers, "Your soul is mine."

Eve passes out on the stool and violently hits her head off the keys on the piano as she falls to the floor. She begins to convulse. Mrs Maztalerz tries to run to Eve's aid, but as soon as she reaches the piano, an unforeseen force awakens around Eve's shaking body and throws Mrs Maztalerz across the stage. Mrs Maztalerz lands in a heap on the ground and lies motionless, her eyes wide open. It's as if her soul is no longer present in her body. Before anyone has chance to tend to both Eve or Mrs Maztalerz, all the lights go off and the theatre becomes dark.

Panicking, the parents begin grabbing their children and fumbling around in the dark. All of them desperately attempt to rush for the nearest exit. When they realise what has happened, all the students behind the stage become hysterical. Everyone starts to scream, and the noise of each scream combined becomes ear-piercing. People of all ages, both young and old, are radiating fear. The evil entity that has taken control of the room is feeding from the distress, gaining strength with every second.

A single spotlight appears at the front of the stage, focused on Eve. Standing up calmly, Jess fixes her attention on Eve. Her eyes hold secrets and are filled with deceit. She looks victorious. Eve is still uncontrollably and violently convulsing on the floor. Black foam begins to ooze from her mouth. Suddenly, the shaking stops and she lies motionless. Jess slowly places one foot in front of the other as she makes her way over to Eve. She is transforming with every inch that she gets closer to Eve's body. Her true demonic form is taking shape.

With the lights off, the parents and children are unaware of the transformation taking place. They continue to climb over one another in a desperate attempt to get out of the building. But as soon as they reach the exits, they realise that all the doors and windows have been locked tight. There's no escape.

Suddenly, the lights flicker back on. Eve is proudly standing at the side of her new owner in all her demonic glory. Raising her arms, Jezebel commands, *"Dormire."*

Every single person in the room, both big and small, instantly falls to the floor. They're frozen stiff. Their eyes are open wide, but it appears as though there is no soul there. Making her way to the exit at the side of Jezebel, Eve says, "You are all lucky I didn't kill you. Your time will come."

Smiling, Jezebel appears happy with Eve's quick acceptance and transition.

Getting up from their chairs in the boardroom, Matthew, Christina, Daniel, Vera, Bill and his nephew Atticus gather their notes from today's meeting. It has gone well, and Bill seems content with the decisions that have been made regarding the finalised advertisement for SaintsVill clothing.

"Atticus, it was great to meet you," says Christina. "I'm sure that, following in your uncle's footsteps, you're going to be a great success."

"Thanks, Christina. Actually, film production has always excited me and so when Uncle Bill invited me to this meeting, there was absolutely no way I was passing up this opportunity."

"Oh, bless you. Well maybe we could get you on an intern here. Matthew, what do you think?"

"Huh?"

"I was saying to Atticus that we could get him on an intern here."

"Oh, yeah, sure."

Bill looks to Matthew. "You alright, Matty lad? You seem tired."

"Huh?"

"I said are you alright, Matty lad?"

This is the second time Matthew's had to answer the same question. Shaking himself, he replies, "Yeah, sorry Bill, I didn't sleep much last night."

"Oh, up all night with a lady caller was you?" Bill says as he winks, nods his head and laughs.

Not wanting to tell the truth, Matthew laughs and replies, "Yeah – something like that."

Smirking, Bill says, "Leave out the seedy details aye, there's young ears about."

Smiling, Matthew looks to Bill's nephew and says, "Yeah, it was nice to meet you, Aaron."

"It's Atticus."

"Oh, sorry, yes, my mistake, it is, isn't it?"

Putting out his hand, Atticus says, "It's been a real pleasure to meet you, Matthew, and I was just saying to Christina how much I admire the film production industry."

"I said he could start an intern here." Christina says.

"Atticus, get Daniel's email address and arrange to come in, this way you can see a day in the life of Honey Productions. You can then decide if you want to start on as an intern with us."

"Aye, Matty boy, you best be coughing up a finder's fee for him, or better still, let's say, a free advertisement. Ha-ha, that should cover it, right?"

"Aye, Bill, is this your secret weapon – get a freebie using this one and keep the wealth? Ha-ha. I tell you what, if he's half as good at business as you are, the lad will be worth every pound."

"You sussed me, Matty boy. I tell you, fine lad is our Atticus. I assure you he's made with great genes. Raised well, aren't you, lad?"

"Thanks, Uncle Bill. I learned from the best."

"You've paid him to say that, haven't you, Bill?" Christina says.

"Aye, cheeky." Putting out his arms, Bill continues, "Christina, come now, bring it in for a hug."

Looking at his watch, Matthew sees the time is 6 p.m. Gathering his things in a rush, he says, "I'm gonna have to shoot. Daniel, don't forget to type the minutes and send them out to everyone. Oh, and pass Aaron, sorry, I mean, Atticus, your email, cause he's going to come in on an intern thing. Right, everyone, it has been a real pleasure, but I must go."

Matthew is in the kitchen, swaying slightly. He's had enough! Like an alcoholic he's drinking straight from the bottle, throwing back gulps of wine. His tie is pulled down and his shirt's hanging out of his pants. No longer resembling the strong man he once was, Matthew looks a mess. His hair's sticking up and his whole appearance is neglected. Slightly drunk from the amount of wine he has consumed in such a short period of time, he stumbles out of the kitchen and begins making his way up the two spiral staircases to his office on the second floor.

He pushes the door open with one arm and waves his bottle of wine around with the other. Matthew sits at the desk and turns the computer on. "Operation bump in the night, ha-ha. I like it. So, now then, now then, now then... what do we have here? I know I turned you on this time, ha, you can't outsmart Matthew Honey," he says, slurring, as he waits for the computer to start up.

Taking another swig of wine, Matthew manages to log in and open up the CCTV camera file. "Now —" he unexpectedly hiccups, "—let us see what's going on then—" another hiccup, "—nanny cam, and, login—" He pauses for another hiccup. The alcohol is clearly having an effect on his system. "Kaboom! CCTV camera. Oh hello, lookie, what is it we have here then! So…" He takes another gulp of his wine from the bottle. "We've decided to play ball this time, have we?"

He clicks the link and the live footage currently recording begins to play. Completely intoxicated, he almost tumbles from his office chair, dramatically waving his arms around. He reaches out to the solid dark-oak cabinet that holds his library of books to steady himself. Laughing hysterically to himself, he says, "Whoopsyyyyy."

He regains his balance and places the virtually empty bottle of wine down on the edge of the desk. Suddenly, he feels a freezing cold draft against the back of his neck, making the hairs on his skin stand to attention. Looking up, he sees the office door is closed, but it's not shut tight. He gets up from his chair and stumbles over to the door, peering through the gap into the dark empty hallway.

"Eve… Jess?"

There's no response. Content that he is, in fact, alone, Matthew ignores the shiver and stumbles back to his desk. Looking at the time on his computer, he sees it's 06.47 p.m. on the 7/7. He has been so distracted that it hasn't registered that he has not spoken to his daughter all day. A look of confusion spreads across his features and he shakes his head as he tries to figure out where he was up to. Reaching for the mouse next to the keyboard he sways slightly, then loses his balance once more. This time he almost knocks the bottle off the edge of the desk as he carelessly begins directing the mouse towards the pre-recorded footage from last night. Rewinding the recording to the time when Eve went to bed, Matthew observes his daughter sleeping, looking her usual angelic and innocent self in her pure white bedsheets. He smiles as he watches her sleeping peacefully. He fast-forwards the recording, Eve's body moving around in her bed at a heightened pace as the hours, minutes and seconds speed by. All looks normal in the room. But no sooner has he begun to feel relieved than something mysterious catches his eye.

He stops the recording at 3.07 a.m. Matthew leans closer to the monitor, staring intently. He can see what looks like smoke seeping around the doorframe. Pressing play once more, he hones in on this spot and watches as the mysterious grey smoke grows thicker and thicker into Eve's room. Matthew sees that his daughter is completely unaware of this presence surrounding her. As the footage continues to play, Matthew is frozen stiff. He can no longer believe what he's seeing. Things like this don't happen in the real world. This is surely wrong; someone has edited the footage as a prank!

Gliding through the closed wooden door, as though the sturdy barrier doesn't even exist, is the same demonic-looking grey woman he's being taunted by in his mind, except this time it isn't in his mind. This recording tells no lies. She's there as clear as day in his daughter's bedroom.

Unsure if he should feel relieved at this confirmation that he's not going insane, or petrified that she is real, Matthew sheds a single silent tear which falls slowly down his face. This image disturbs him so much it literally shocks the alcohol out of his system and pushes him right back to being sober. Watching as the events unfold, he sees her true horrific form; he sees her grey body and her long black hair which is dripping a black substance everywhere she steps.

Suddenly, Matthew sees Eve's sleeping body shoot up. Eve sits up straight in her bed, her eyes wide open. Once again, Matthew leans closer to the monitor, with a look of regret and horror on his face. He sees Eve is no longer Eve. She's a mini mirror reflection of this demonic entity. Her eyes resemble gaping black holes and black blood oozes from around her eye sockets. Her skin has turned an unearthly shade of grey and rips have formed all over her body, with black blood pulsing out of each one.

Trying to come to terms with the horrific image of his daughter, Matthew slumps back in his office chair when suddenly a huge, black raven appears on screen. This sinful-looking creature lands on Eve's shoulder and begins pecking at her face. Eve doesn't flinch or react to this. The grey demonic entity makes her way from the doorway across to Eve to join her evil acquaintance. With the raven on one side, the demonic entity leans over to Eve's face and with her black tongue she licks and begins ingesting the substance oozing from Eve's existence.

Matthew feels a vibration on the table. It becomes repetitive and rhythmic. The demonic entity's mouth is moving. Sitting up in bed, Eve appears to be embracing the words spoken. He rewinds the footage and turns the volume to its highest point. Through the distorted recording he struggles to hear the words she speaks, but he can make out a tune. Grabbing his headphones from the drawer, he plugs these in and once again presses play. Closing his eyes, Matthew hears it! It's a nursery rhyme. With a dulcet and eerie tone, he hears the demonic entity singing Ring a' Ring o' Roses, but the words aren't quite right. Fiddling with the settings, Matthew rewinds the footage and listens again. This time he hears, "Ring a' Ring o' Roses – your soul is mine. Ring a' Ring o' Roses – you've been chosen for the dark side."

The rhyme sparks a sense of familiarity. He's heard it before. Continuing to watch in disbelief, Matthew feels numb. The raven suddenly flaps her huge wings and goes out of sight. The demonic entity looks straight to the door, appearing startled. A sudden transformation begins to take place. Holding his breath, Matthew can't believe his eyes. He can't process what he's seeing. It's her... it's...

"Matthew, what are you doing?"

Matthew jumps out of his skin, this time successfully knocking the wine bottle off the desk and onto the floor. He looks like he's just seen a ghost. His eyes are open wide and he's breathing at a rapid rate, frozen stiff to his chair.

Standing in the doorway, Jess once again speaks. "Matthew, what's wrong?"

"Jess... I... Erm..."

"You what?"

With his voice low and his eyes still wide he says, "Where's Eve?"

Looking to the monitor on the desk, she smirks as she makes her way closer to him. "So, now you know."

"Where is she, where is my daughter?"

"Don't you worry. I told you, Mr Honey, I always take good care of my pieces. Evelyn Jade, come here, please."

Entering the office, Eve stands directly at the side of Jess.

"Eve, come here, get away from her. Get away from her now!"

Matthew tries to stand but realises he's stuck to his chair. "Please, I beg you, don't do this; she's all I have."

"You see, that's the problem, she's actually all you never had. I selected you from billions of souls. I mapped out your fate. I created your destiny. You should know something, Mr Honey. I might as well tell you, now that the truth is out. I have been watching you for years – many, many, many years. Your first and only born, Evelyn Jade, way before she was even conceived, had been chosen for a great purpose. She was always a possession of mine. Did you think it was a coincidence that you chose that gift for Lauren all those years ago - the solid silver locket from the old gypsy lady's stall? Did you think I turned up wearing one almost identical to it by chance?"

Choosing not to answer Jess's question, Matthew's desperate to get his daughter away from this evil individual. "Eve, come here, please. Eve, listen to my voice. It's me, your dad."

"Fuck you, Mr Honey and your innocence, or should I say your desperate and weak mind. You see, you were so obsessed with your dead wife that you totally missed all the signs. I'm calculated, but you're stupid. You've made this so very easy for me. I couldn't have you taking off with my chosen one. The locket your wife fell so desperately in love with, it was my hunter, my tracker, so to speak. I have always been watching, watching every single move you've each made. You see, I always knew I was up against one teeny tiny problem…"

Matthew looks at Eve, who stands still in the doorway. Her skin tone is slowly changing to a slight shade of grey. Jess makes her way over to Matthew and leans into his ear. Her breath is ice-cold and smells pungent. It leaves a strong metallic taste at the back of his throat, making him feel nauseous.

"Unfortunately," Jess continues, "you both got too attached to something that never belonged you. I was faced with a dilemma, so to speak. I was faced with the fact that my possession, my creation, my chosen soul, had two very strong keepers who loved her very much, and so I decided that one of you had to go. Yes! It was I who killed your poor little Lauren. It was I who ripped your world apart and made you weak and vulnerable. Now, Mr Honey, I'm taking what's rightfully mine! Did you really think you could keep her from me? Ha! I killed your wife and you're lucky that I don't kill you too, now that you've served your purpose. The clock is ticking. My demonic empire will be unleashed upon the world. I am the Dark Empress and the universe will be mine. This is just the beginning," she says, standing up straight and re-joining Eve.

Silent tears fall rapidly down Matthew's motionless face as he realises what she's saying. It's worse than he could have ever imagined. All his worst fears and nightmares are coming true.

"I am Jezebel. And she is mine. Now, let's have some fun. Do you like to play games, Mr Honey? Ring a' Ring o' Roses…"

As these words leave her lips, Jezebel and Eve begin showcasing their horrific true demonic forms. Cracks appear in Eve's grey skin and a black, thick substance begins to drip from them and out of her mouth. She coughs and the thick substance rolls down her chin and onto her chest.

The silver necklace and heart-shaped locket hanging around Eve's neck is enveloped by the sticky slime, destroying the beauty that this item once possessed. The weight of it hangs heavy and the chain snaps, the treasured piece of jewellery falling to the floor. The final piece of the puzzle, the final item to remind Eve of the life she once had, has now gone! As it lands on the floor, the Dark Empress and her chosen soul are united at last, standing strong side by side. With their transformation complete, the pair throw themselves at Matthew and begin dragging his soul deeper and deeper into the dark abyss of his own mind.

The time has come; it's the final game.

CHAPTER SIXTEEN

The Final Game

"Eve… Eve… Eve!"

"Yes, Dad?"

"Eve – where are you?"

"I'm here."

"*Where?* I can't see anything."

"Dad…"

"Listen to me, princess, I don't want you to panic, just follow my voice. I'm coming to find you and we're going to get out of here together and go home."

"Help me, please, save me, you must before it's too—"

"Eve? Eve! Before it's too what?"

As the echoes of his voice disappear, the silence becomes deafening. Matthew is desperate to hear his daughter's voice. Holding hope in his heart that she's still nearby he shouts out, "Darling, everything's going to be all right. I'm coming to find you."

He is alone and completely surrounded by darkness, unaware that he's been trapped inside the darkest depths of his own mind. His fear taking over, Matthew feels exposed and vulnerable. He bravely takes one step forward, hearing only the sound of his breath as it leaves his body.

Suddenly he feels an excruciating pain in his wrists. An unseen force is cutting through his soft flesh as his arms are mysteriously ripped apart and raised above his head. Screaming out in agony, he is forcefully pulled off his feet. He comes to an abrupt halt and is left dangling from what he can only imagine is a great height. He feels the same excruciating pain in his ankles as they are also ripped apart and restrained in the same manner. Unable to see who, or what, is doing this to him, Matthew struggles to free himself. But the fiercer he pulls, the tighter the grip becomes.

He gives in and stays still. The movement creates too much pain for him to bear. Matthew drops his head. His energy levels are low. There is an eerie silence, but he doesn't feel alone. The dark energy embedded in this still place begins toying with his thoughts. With his sight gone, his hearing becomes strong. His ears twitch as a tune circulates inside his mind, taking over his thoughts. The haunting, eerie version of Ring a' Ring o' Roses is being hummed repeatedly.

"Do you like to play games, Mr Honey?" a voice suddenly says.

"Why are you doing this to us? Where is she? Eve, Eve!" Matthew shouts out, desperate to free himself and not engage in these torturous mind games.

"Wrong answer, Mr Honey. I hope you're ready. Let the games begin."

Intimidating, insane laughter circulates in his mind alongside the incessant nursery tune. Suddenly a spotlight lights his surroundings. As his sight adjusts to the brightness, Matthew takes in his unfortunate situation. He's suspended inside a huge spider's web made of thick rope. As he struggles, attempting again to free himself, he hears Eve's desperate cry: "Dad, help me."

Looking down, he sees Eve dressed in her mother's nightie, on her knees, helplessly staring up at him. Reaching out she says, "Please, I'm dying."

"Eve! No, I will not lose you, don't worry, I'm coming, darling."

As soon as these words leave his mouth he fights with all his might against the ropes that bind him. The web begins to shake violently. Peering up above his head, Matthew sees evil, blood-red eyes approaching from the darkness. Attached to these sinister-looking eyes is a thick-legged tarantula the size of a t-rex. Tripping over its long legs as it makes its way rapidly towards Matthew, the monstrous creature spits venom. Before he has time to react Matthew hears, "*Mi temono.*"

He is instantly released from his entrapment and falls once again into the darkness. He lands in a heap and curls up. Rocking back and forth, he firmly holds his head in both his hands in pain, his skull having smashed off the ground as he landed. Petrified of the unknown, he screams out loud with agony. He's confused, frantic. He tries to allow his mind to process what's happening. He pats his body to ensure he's in one piece and searches his surroundings, not realising that his wrists and ankles are wounded, and blood is gushing out.

"Eve, where are you, darling?"

Night has fallen and not a single star can be seen. It's as though he is lost deep within the universe. His surroundings are dimly lit by streetlamps. It's freezing cold. Matthew can see his breath leaving his body. He hears the chiming of bells and sees the outline of a cathedral across the way. A castle stands alongside. The desperate cries of his daughter begin to echo alongside the vibration of the chimes. Matthew looks up high at the ruins of the castle and sees Eve at a broken window. She's calling out to him: "Help me, I want to go home."

"I'm coming for you, darling, stay there."

"Hurry, she's coming for me."

Without so much as a second thought for his own safety, or indeed his life, Matthew runs towards the castle and attempts to force his way through the huge wooden door with its steel fixtures and bolts. He's unsuccessful, but that's not going to stop him. Running around to the other side of the castle, Matthew is confronted with another challenge: an unsteady, manmade grey-brick wall stands before him, supported by a thick, razor-sharp metal fence that is almost half the height of the castle. He throws himself at it, the metal clinking as Matthew grips onto the gaps and begins fearlessly climbing, one leg after the other. Like a rocket he launches himself over the top. The razor-sharp metal rips through the layers of his clothing and gouges deep into the flesh on his leg. He falls from the top onto the ground on the other side. With adrenaline surging through his veins, he doesn't notice the blood gushing from his head and limbs.

Stumbling up onto his feet, Matthew refuses to give up. He feels an electrical, powerful surge of energy as he charges at the castle, determined to save his daughter and break free. Scaling the wall of this huge structure, he finally makes it high enough to throw himself through one of the unprotected gaping holes on the side of the castle.

Matthew is finally inside. His heart is racing. He may be inside, but now he's got an even bigger challenge on his hands: he's got to find his daughter in this haunted-looking building, and he doesn't think for a second it's going to be easy. The only tiny glimmer of light comes from the streetlamps outside.

Matthew's current physical state has become somewhat life-threatening. He's rapidly losing blood and his body is getting weaker with every second that passes. But his attention is fixed on finding his daughter. His heart is strong and the love he has for her is empowering him enough to ignore his body's signals and keep fighting.

"Eve? Eve? Where are you, darling?"

"Dad, I'm here."

Following the sound of her voice, he frantically runs around the castle.

"Eve?"

"I'm over here."

He trips over his feet, struggling to keep up with himself. Finally, Matthew reaches the room where he hears her voice. Without any hesitation, he rushes down the grey-brick stairs. His feet kick debris, which bounces down the steps. The sound of the crumbling falling rocks echoes throughout the castle. The internal structure of this historical building isn't as sturdy as it looks. With his heart racing, Matthew peers into the dark, empty stone-walled room. One streak of light beams in from the streetlamp outside. He closes his eyes and breathes in deeply, on his exhale, with his voice low, he says, "Eve?"

"Here, Dad."

"Eve, oh, my princess, there you are."

Matthew walks into the room, turns and sees Eve. She's cowering in a dark corner. He runs over and bursts into tears as he reaches out to comfort and hold his daughter. But before he can take her in his arms an unforeseen force awakens and throws him to the other side of the room, well away from the exit. She's gone. Jumping up with shock, Matthew attempts to run, but realises he can't. He hears an unfamiliar, spine-shivering, daunting voice say, "Ring a' Ring o' Roses – I've been chosen for the dark side."

Looking to his left, Matthew sees Eve. She's still wearing only her mother's nightie, which is covered in grey dust, dirt and rips. She's slowly crawling down the same stairs he's just walked upon himself, singing, "Ring a' Ring o' Roses."

She stops and looks towards Matthew. Staring directly at him, her head tilted, with a deep voice that doesn't sound like her own she says, "Are you scared, Mr Honey? Is this better?"

Feeling physically sick but unable to throw up, Matthew hears a crack as she abruptly snaps her own neck. With her head hanging low, she says, "Help me."

Her body rises off the step, levitating up high. Her eyes are as black as the midnight sky and sit as gaping holes in her face. Eve is no longer Eve. She's a true demonic reflection of the sadistic owner of her soul. Her body dangles in mid-air and begins jolting and twitching, her bones dislocating one by one. A black, thick substance gushes out of her mouth, lands on the floor and travels towards Matthew.

"Help me."

She lets out an insane laugh as the entity that's taken ownership of Eve drags her closer to him. Frozen stiff and attempting to process what's taking place before his eyes, Matthew is unable to blink. His chest is rapidly moving up and down, his breathing erratic and out of sync. His heart feels as though, at any minute, it's going to pop.

"Help me – Ring a' Ring o' Roses."

With these final words, Eve violently throws herself at her dad.

His mind spinning out of control, Matthew screams out loud… and is released from his entrapment and thrown directly into another.

Getting weaker by the second as he's still rapidly losing blood, Matthew reluctantly looks around. He's surrounded by crispy autumn-coloured leaves which are smothered with dirt. Not a building can be seen, just tree after tree after tree. The sky is black and there's not a single star in sight. A grey mist appears, circulating around the sturdy trees. It quickly covers the ground he sits on and rises to his neck. Slowly stumbling onto his feet, Matthew attempts to hold himself up. He leans against a tree trunk, trying to catch his breath. This deceitful mist is entering into his body, attacking his organs and suffocating him internally. Matthew begins to pant uncontrollably. His back against the tree he huffs, "Eve."

The mist has a nauseating stench of death, and he almost falls back down to the ground as he retches.

His eyes closed, he hears the crunching of the leaves in the distance, then getting louder and louder. Matthew is taking no chances. He hobbles in the opposite direction, trying to get as far away from whoever is making the noise as he possibly can. The trees all look the same. The branches begin pulling at his arms, scratching his face. One twig catches his eye. Blinded, he falls to the floor. As soon as he lands, the impure branches wrap around Matthew's body and tightly restrain him. Slowly drifting in and out of consciousness, Matthew lies half-dead. The sound of the crunching leaves and snapping twigs has stopped.

"So, now do you like to play games, Mr Honey?"

Without a single molecule of energy left within his body, Matthew lies motionless. His breathing is slow and his eyes remain half-open.

"Shame, I thought you might have put up a little more of fight than this. I must say, even your wife was a stronger adversary than this. Pathetic."

Slowly making her way around his body, Jezebel, in her true demonic form, is teasing his soul. The grey mist is getting thicker and thicker, surrounding Matthew until he can no longer see what's in front of him.

Suddenly the mist disappears. Through the narrow slits of his eyes, Matthew sees Eve. She is once again Eve. Precious, innocent and pure. Tears form in the corners of his eyes, spilling over and falling down his face. Slowly he whispers, "Eve…"

With a glow surrounding her, she resembles an angel. Matthew's levels of strength and life gradually begins to rise. His heart warms at this vision. He begins to question deep in his mind. His decision is made. He isn't going to give up and let this evil woman win. There's no way she's ripping his life apart anymore. Clenching his fists together and tightening all his muscles, Matthew groans as he stretches out and rips all the strangulating branches from his body. Jezebel looks on, smiling deceitfully as he uses up the last of his life's energy on a pointless task. Freeing himself, Matthew stumbles onto his feet and feebly makes his way towards his daughter. But as soon as he gets within reaching distance she disappears, and Jezebel stands before him. Reaching out to Matthew, she violently throws herself at him and drags him toward his death.

Then there is nothing.

Matthew comes around. He is unable to move his body. He sees he is lying alone on Lauren's grave.

Then the darkness takes over again and he's out.

Matthew wakes to the beep of machinery. He looks down at his body and sees he is bandaged and bruised. The room is dimly lit and he's wearing a hospital gown in a hospital bed. Looking to his body once more, he notices all the wires and machines that are attached to him. Taking these off one by one, he hears the machines begin to beep frantically as they lose their readings. Suddenly, two nurses burst into the room.

"No, no, no, you mustn't do that; just lie back, please."

"Eve, but Eve…"

"You can see Eve when you're better."

"I must… I need… I have to…"

"That's all well and good, Matthew, but at the moment you're too unwell to do anything. Now lie back, please."

She injects him with a sedative. Matthew slowly begins to drift off. The last words he hears are from the nurse.

"Who's Eve? Do we have a contact number on his records?"

"No, we can't find any contacts on his records."

CHAPTER SEVENTEEN

You've Been Here Before

The house is no longer a home. All the curtains are closed. Neglected and filthy, the Honey residence resembles a derelict building. The walls are dirty, the contents are smashed to pieces and the only item that stands strong is the golden mirror that was once proudly placed at the bottom of the stairs. The paint is chipped throughout the house and the carpet is black from dirt. The property is unrecognisable.

The day room is dark, dim and daunting. The mirror stands against the closed curtains at the front window. Matthew sits in a wooden rocking chair, slowly rocking back and forth, back and forth.

Wearing dirty, faded, black ripped jeans and black boots that are thick with dust, Matthew is unrecognisable from the strong man he once was. With his head tilted to the side, he resembles a sedated mental patient.

Looking at his hands in the mirror, Matthew gently smirks as he sees what he's holding. In one hand he has a 9mm pistol with a sleek black silencer. In the other hand he holds a golden picture frame. The image inside the frame is of the family he once had. Matthew Honey, Evelyn Jade Honey and Lauren Honey. The Honeys. How sweet their life once was, but no more.

Hanging from the picture frame is the locket that both Lauren and Eve once wore. The hunter.

"Whatever my fate, I ask you to free me. If death is in my cards, please let my soul know she's gone with no return. If life is in my cards, please let my soul live free and tell me how I can bring her back."

Continuing to rock, Matthew is no longer Matthew. He's a broken man at the depths of despair, with nothing left to live for except the hope that one day he'll be reunited with his daughter; she is still living, after all. And what does he have to lose? The only thing to fear is death, and death doesn't seem so bad given his current cursed life.

"I will find her…"

His rocking gets faster and faster as he looks in the mirror and says, "I won't lose you, Eve."

He lets out an insane laugh. The room suddenly goes dark as he shouts, "So you want to play games, do you? Let the hunt begin. I'm coming for you, Jezebel. Eve, I promise on my life this time I won't let you down."

The insane laughter continues… And so, the hunt begins…

Until next time…

ABOUT THE AUTHOR

A.L. Frances is a thirty-two-year-old British author.

The Broken is the first book of a four-part series and marks A.L. Frances' debut in literary fiction.

Born in Wythenshawe, South Manchester, she is the product of a broken home. Her formal education was cut short before she could gain any qualifications and she became a mother to three children by the time she was just twenty years old. At twenty-one A.L. Frances suddenly finds herself cast in the role of a single parent, destined to repeat the cycle of her own difficult upbringing.

Determined to give her children a better start in life, she moved to the countryside village of Hollingworth, and eventually settled into a career in law. It was during this transition that she found herself on a journey of self-discovery. Attending multiple mindset enhancing seminars in England, America and Canada, she was exposed to the tutelage of inspirational speakers such as Bob Proctor, Tony Robbins, and Mel Robbins among others. A.L. Frances was eventually introduced to Peggy McColl, a New York Times Best Selling Author. Standing on the stage, Peggy said the words that would inspire her into action. Peggy said, "Everyone has a book in them." as she pointed into the crowd. It was at this point that A.L. Frances fell in love with the idea of writing her own book and telling her own story; one that would address one of her biggest fears: the vulnerabilities of broken homes.

At the age of twenty-nine, A.L. Frances decided it was time to start the next chapter of her life.

What follows is the start of her journey…

Printed in Great Britain
by Amazon

43456278R00111